CANYON WAR

Doc Beck Westerns Book 1

SARAH ELISABETH SAWYER

ROCKHAVEN PUBLISHING

RockHaven Publishing
P.O. Box 1103
Canton, Texas 75103

Editors: Lynda Kay Sawyer, Catherine Frappier, Natalie Bright
Cover Design: Mollie E. Reeder
Author Photo by R. A. Whiteside. Courtesy of the National Museum of the
American Indian, Smithsonian Institution

Paperback ISBN: 978-0-9910259-7-8

PROLOGUE

The night sounds in the Palo Duro Canyon were deafening. Thunderous katydid and cricket chirps echoed off the walls and up to the rim where Clem Baxter stood. He could hardly hear his own thoughts for all the racket. But he preferred the clatter of night critters to his brother's low grumbling.

Woodrow Baxter stood slightly behind him, right where Clem wanted the second oldest son of the Baxter Ranch. Clem was the oldest and now head of the family of four brothers. Woodrow was next in line if anything happened to him, Kurt next, then Van. Of the three, Clem would pick Van. Woodrow and Kurt were too soft.

He could hear Woodrow shifting his feet despite the night sounds croaking up from the canyon.

"Clem, I'm not going against you on this, even though I don't think it's altogether right. But there's no point in waiting for the Lowells to show up. Let's set off the charge now and get out of here."

"Pa always said you were yellow, a bad influence on Kurt."

Clem didn't have to turn to know his brother stiffened. But Woodrow wouldn't dare go up against him, no more than he would their father, barely cold in his grave.

Pa had left Clem, his oldest son, in charge of the Baxter Ranch when he passed of a rattlesnake bite he'd gotten in that very canyon. They were returning home after a confrontation with the Lowell family. The patriarch was in such a state he hadn't been aware of the danger until it struck.

Clem heard Woodrow pivot on his boot heel and clomp away toward their horses. Good. As long as he kept Woodrow off-balance, he kept him under his thumb. Clem was a little off-balance himself after the swig of whiskey he'd taken before they rode out to the canyon, but that didn't affect his judgment or his rightful place.

His other two brothers, Van and Kurt, came up to him. Kurt was the spindly twenty-two-year-old who took after Woodrow too much. The Baxters were supposed to be a tough lot, feared and respected in the area for their fierce determination to build the largest spread around the canyon, no matter who got crushed in the process. Like the Lowells.

The Baxters were a long way from that goal, and Woodrow and Kurt added black marks to the family's reputation.

Kurt whispered, "Clem, can I wait with the horses when it's time?"

Clem rounded on him, making Kurt take a step back. Pa had demonstrated that if he couldn't earn the respect of someone, he'd force it from them. In the light of the full moon, Kurt's gaunt face was drawn and pale. He'd never grow up.

Clem said, "You keep whining, and I'll have you set the charge off instead of helping Van do it."

Van, the youngest and quickest tempered of the four, took a step forward. He was short, brown-haired and eyed like their father, and with enough aggressiveness to do whatever he needed to, but with barely enough smarts to keep it in check. "You said I could set off the charge, Clem. Pa wouldn't let you go back on your word."

Clem glared at him. "Don't be telling me what Pa would or wouldn't do." He turned his authoritative gaze on Kurt. "And you're going to do what I say, even if it kills you."

Kurt rubbed his palms up and down his trouser legs, looking bare without the six-gun Clem expected him to have. He didn't push it, not even on this night, not since Kurt had nearly blown off one of his own toes trying to follow Clem's orders to quick draw and shoot tin cans a day after they buried their father.

Kurt couldn't handle himself worth a rock, but Clem was going to make a man out of him yet, same as their father had been trying for ten years. The Baxter boys were expected to become men at a young age to survive in the Texas Panhandle.

Woodrow joined them again. "Someone does need to stay with the horses when the ruckus starts, Clem. Why don't you let Kurt instead of me—"

Clem gripped the butt of his revolver, a threatening gesture their father had often used when the boys got too big for the belt. He had pistol-whipped Clem more than once.

"He'll do just what I say," Clem growled. "You all will."

Van's head jerked to the right, squinting in the moonlight to the canyon floor. Clem gritted his teeth. His brothers had distracted him from keeping a sharp ear to distinguish the canyon sounds from invaders. The Lowells and their stinking sheep were coming up the canyon eight hundred feet below where the Baxters stood. Them Lowells thought they could sneak by in the cover of darkness.

Clem hissed at his brothers, "Don't just stand there like fools. Get in position, but Van, don't set off that charge until I give the signal."

Van slapped Kurt's arm and darted off and over the rim on the narrow trail. Kurt followed, kicking up dust like Clem had warned them not to. Clem met Woodrow's eyes, his brother standing a half head taller than him. But Pa said the size of a man didn't matter. He just needed to keep an edge over Woodrow.

"You get back and stay with the horses. Home's a long walk from here."

Woodrow didn't move, holding Clem's gaze longer than he should have. But he broke away in the nick of time and headed down to where the Baxters had corralled their horses among a half-moon of boulders.

Clem released his grip on his six-gun and edged to the canyon rim. He got down and crawled the rest of the way forward, removing his hat and stilling himself to get in tune with the night sounds and hone in on the sight of the Lowell men afoot, driving their sheep through the rugged terrain of the Palo Duro. They were trying to sneak through a passageway to the corral and cabin set up at the other end in an offshoot of the canyon. There was a spring down there and patches of green grass this time of year. The Lowells intended to use it despite Clem's warning that the Baxter patriarch had claimed use of it two years ago.

Settlers and ranchers had been scrapping over grazing rights in the 60-mile long canyon for some time. The Baxters had their territory staked, and no sheepherder settlers were going to infringe on it.

Clem waited, taking his breath in and holding it. If they set off the charge too soon, they would fail to catch the lead sheep in the rockslide. Too late, and they would catch the Lowell bunch in the slide. Clem wouldn't mind seeing them all buried, but his pa had warned him that dead bodies brought lawmen circling like buzzards.

Clem glanced to his right where Van squatted next to the blasting machine to set off the dynamite. They'd strategically placed it before dark on the wall of the canyon, behind enough large rocks to block the passageway. The Baxters had another way into that section of the canyon that the Lowells didn't know about. This would be enough to stop them from ever finding it.

Clem looked for Kurt and swore under his breath when he saw him huddled a good fifteen feet back from Van. He told Kurt to stay close in case there were any problems and to watch for the signal to give to Van. Kurt wasn't even looking at him. He was watching the canyon floor. So was Van.

Clem hissed, "Hey!"

Neither brother heard him, intent on watching the approaching sheep as the Lowells came around the final bend before the passageway.

Relying on the night noises and baying of the sheep echoing up from the canyon, Clem hissed louder, "Hey!"

Kurt's head jerked, and Clem flagged with his hat. Even in the darkness, Clem could see Kurt's eyes go wide as he realized his negligence. He bolted forward and said something to Van. Immediately, Van shoved the handle down on the blasting machine and the entire canyon seemed to explode.

The solid rock of the rim beneath Clem shook violently, and he used his hat to cover his head as a spray of rocks rained over him. The smell of dusty earth and stale sweat choked him, but he kept his head down until the shaking stopped and the rocky rain quit falling.

Ears ringing, he scrambled to his feet, dizzy and more unsteady than he wanted his brothers to see. But none of them were in sight.

Clem scooted over the edge of the rim, catching himself on hardwood shrubs to keep from sliding over the edge and the eight hundred foot drop below. But he wasn't looking for his brothers, not yet. First, he had to see if they'd been successful.

Through the haze of gray dust, he made out the landscape that he was so familiar with. More than twice the amount of rock he'd figured had shot off the wall and rumbled to the floor. It rested there, along with tons of other rock that had bounced loose in the wake of the larger boulders.

The passageway was sealed.

Clem wished he had more light, but from what he could see, a remnant of the sheep herd was running mad away from the slide, braying in high-pitched tones. Clem smiled. Dumb sheep, just like their owners.

But where were their owners?

He scanned the canyon and saw movement not belonging to the critters. The Lowells were chasing after the sheep, echoes of their shouts reaching Clem. One of the men below halted and turned. Though Clem was hidden in the shadow of the rim above him, he felt the man's gaze, loaded with hate, land on him. In the dark, Clem recognized Sam Lowell, the oldest son of the Lowell clan. Sam would know the rockslide was no accident.

He and Clem had come to blows on their last encounter, right before Pa was snake bit. Clem would settle that score eventually. For now, the destruction of half the sheep herd was enough, and more than one of their men was limping. Looked like one was carrying another man slung over his shoulder.

Once Clem was certain they were fleeing and not making an attempt to climb the steep wall in a blind rage, he turned his gaze to the ledge where his two brothers had been. The blasting machine was there, but Van and Kurt weren't.

Clem couldn't reach the ledge from where he was, so he climbed back up to the rim and went to the next ledge, Woodrow coming behind him. Clem turned on him.

"I told you to stay with the horses."

Woodrow didn't back down. "Are you deaf? I heard Van hollering for help."

Clem itched to backhand his brother, same as their father would've done if Woodrow talked to him that way. But he'd save that fight for another time. He did hear Van calling now.

The two oldest Baxter brothers scrambled down the narrow trail that the younger ones had taken to reach the ledge. Van limped toward them, half dragging Kurt with one arm slung over his shoulder. Kurt looked dead, but Clem saw him move his feet in an effort to walk with Van.

Woodrow rushed to Kurt's other side and quickly wrapped his brother's arm around his shoulder, lifting him from the ground and stumbling forward. Clem backed up the trail, talking to Van.

"What happened?"

A stream of blood ran down the side of Van's face, but true to Baxter form, he didn't complain.

"That explosion knocked me off my feet. Sent me over the edge. Kurt pulled me up, but the ledge gave way, and he tumbled down aways. Didn't you hear me hollering?"

Clem kept backing up the ledge, feeling for his footing as he went, not wanting to show any weakness before his three brothers.

"You did good. You all did good. Let's get Kurt home and fixed up."

Right when they topped the rim, Kurt screamed and his back jerked. Van and Woodrow couldn't hold onto him with the convulsions and quickly lowered him to the ground. Kurt arched, gripping his back and crying. Pa never would put up with crying from his sons, no matter how bad they were hurt. But there was something in Kurt's screams that chilled Clem to the bone.

Van stood back, wiping blood from his eyes with his dirty shirt sleeve. Woodrow gripped Kurt, pinning him to the ground and holding him still. He looked up at Clem, eyes wide. It was the first time Woodrow had looked at him for direction, and Clem snapped into action. He pointed at Van with his hat.

"Ride into Amarillo and bring a doctor back to the ranch house. Don't get that town doctor that didn't treat Pa right. There's some special doctor there that was helping out with measles they had in town. Called Doc Beck. Bring him. And don't go into town alone. Pick up that Jimmy kid and take him with you."

Van spat blood. "Town's 20 miles from the ranch house."

"Hell's closer if you'd rather go there. Otherwise, get riding."

CHAPTER 1

L ate night knocking always meant trouble for Rebekah LaRoche. But she'd rather be needed at all hours than not wanted at all.

The hammering at the Garland house front door continued as Rebekah threw her robe over her nightgown. She entered the dark front room, drawn curtains not allowing in the moonlight. But staying in this house the past three weeks gave her the ability to navigate between the sofa and wingback chair that stood before the fireplace.

She'd let the fire die down with evening, though springs in Amarillo could be chilly. She preferred a slight nip in the air at night, finding it gave her deeper sleep and alertness when she needed it. She needed it now.

Rebekah had checked her small pocket watch when the pounding started and noted it was 1:10 a.m. She tucked the watch in her robe and peeked sideways through the closed curtain over the glass window of the front door. The Garland's home wasn't ornate, but it was a fine place to stay while they were out of town and gave her quiet reprieve from the hospital each day.

Rebekah suspected someone from the hospital had sent for her, but the continuous knocking was so rude, her instincts told her this was a different sort calling on her.

Through the tiny split in the curtains over the door, Rebekah could see a scrawny sandy-haired boy standing on the porch. He wore a purple bandana and had his hands sunk in his short tan jacket pockets, showing the six-gun he wore.

Rebekah shifted the other way as the pounding stopped. Another young man, older than the first and shorter, stood outside the door, a scowl on his face. He looked undecided, then raised his hand as if to rap again.

Rebekah unlocked the door and swung it open, causing him to hit air.

"Excuse me, young man, but you will soon have every dog in town barking."

She took note of the caked-over cut on his forehead partly covered by his hat. Her heart softened. "Is there some sort of emergency here?"

His voice was dry and husky as he said, "We're looking for Doc Beck."

"I'm Doctor Rebekah LaRoche."

His uncertain expression deepened. "But you're a woman."

"And you're a keen observer. Now, what is the emergency?"

The young man stared at her, dumbfounded. The sandy-haired boy, situated behind him, stepped forward.

His eyes were just as wide in shock, but he stammered, "Ma'am, we got a hurt man out at the Baxter Ranch. We need a doctor, bad."

Rebekah eyed the two. "You will need to bring him into the hospital. I don't make house calls in the middle of the night with strange young men."

The boy started to respond, but the other cut in. "If you're a doctor, then you're gonna come take care of my brother. Right now."

There weren't many good reasons Rebekah could think of why these young men didn't want to go to the established town doctor. But they did seem genuine in their concern. They looked exhausted and scared beneath their stout demeanor.

Still, she held her ground. "As I said, you need to go to the hospital or town doctor. I'm only passing through and will be leaving on the afternoon train—"

"You're coming with us right now!"

The young man's hand went to his six-gun, gripping the handle and partly pulling it from the holster. The sandy-haired boy put out a hand to block his arm.

"Van, you can't draw down on a woman!"

"Shut up, Jimmy. This gal is gonna do what I say, or I'll blow her head off."

Rebekah kept a firm grip on the door handle, her hand tingling. She could slam and lock the door and possibly get to her bag in the bedroom before they broke through, but that wasn't her smartest move. She still had some diplomacy left to try.

Taking a deep breath in outward resignation, she said, "Since you put it that way...I am a doctor, and it sounds like someone needs help. I'll get dressed and come with you."

"You'll come with us like you are," Van said.

Rebekah scowled at him, but she knew to pick her battles. This wasn't it. She stepped out on the porch in the cool night air and crossed her arms while keeping her gentile posture.

"I will need my medical bag."

Van shoved his revolver back into his holster and nodded at Jimmy. "Get it. Quick."

Rebekah sighed. "It's in the bedroom to the left at the foot of the bed."

Jimmy met her eyes, looking apologetic as he smiled a little. He couldn't be more than fifteen or sixteen with that baby face. He dodged inside and came back a minute later with her bag. Rebekah started to take it, but he held it close.

"I'll carry it for you, ma'am. It's awful heavy."

"Tools of my profession."

They would never guess what lay in the bottom that added so much extra weight.

CHAPTER 2

In her many years of life—thirty-four to be exact—Rebekah had endured all sorts of rough traveling. Even at a young age, from being born in a teepee in Nebraska to living in a log cabin on the Omaha Reservation, she had known she would be someone on the move. Although after medical school, she'd expected to settle down in one location to practice. But she often found patients couldn't come to her. She had to go to them.

Now that she was no longer allowed home on the reservation, she found herself on the move more times than not.

Still, she wouldn't mind admitting the unpleasantness of riding behind the saddle, clinging to a boy as they rode full gallop in the dark across the Texas Panhandle as the cold night air ripped through her robe and nightgown. Rebekah could think of far better ways of traveling.

When they finally pulled up in front of a ranch-style house, she decided against making any remarks on how stiff and cold she was.

The boy, Jimmy, swung his leg over his horse's neck and jumped to the ground. The horse shied, and Rebekah gripped the cantle to keep from falling off. Jimmy turned and held his hands up as though to swing her down. Instead, she pulled herself forward into the seat, found the stirrup, and dismounted.

Jimmy kept his hands out as if waiting to catch her, but grinned when she turned to face him. "You've ridden astride before, ma'am."

"More times than you have, I would wager, young man."

He kept grinning as he untied her medical bag from the horn of his saddle.

Van ran up the steps of the house and started to plow into the door when it swung open. The man in the doorway caught Van by the shoulders to steady him, though he looked unsteady himself.

"About time you got back."

"How's Kurt?"

"Bad."

Rebekah took her bag from Jimmy and climbed the steps in the light from the lamp shining through the door. The man in the doorway jerked back and eyed her up and down. It was always surprising for people to see a woman doctor. But she'd never had to overcome this prejudice in her night robe, and with a man who was hitting the bottle hard. That never helped any situation.

"I understand you have an injured man here," she said.

The man looked between her and Van, his jaw shifting in disbelief and, if Rebekah read him right, boiling anger barely contained. His eyes were bloodshot from the whiskey she smelled on him.

Van spoke fast. "Clem, this is the doc you wanted me to bring back. Doc Beck."

Clem glared at him. "I didn't tell you to bring a woman here. And a Mexican woman at that." Clem stared at her. "Or something. What are you, anyway?"

"I'm a doctor."

"She has a funny last name," Van said.

Clem's dark brown eyes were tinged red, like smoldering coal.

He opened his mouth to say something, but a yell behind him cut him off. It sounded like a wounded animal, but Rebekah knew from her years of practicing medicine that this was a human in pain.

A voice came from inside the house, "Hold still, Kurt! Stop trying to get up."

"Where's Clem?" A trembling voice croaked.

Rebekah knew it was her patient and that she was capable of helping him. But she held herself from forcing her way inside.

Clem looked behind him toward the voices, then back at Rebekah. It wouldn't be the first time someone refused to allow her to treat their loved one.

Rebekah calmly gestured to her medical bag. "I'm ready to do what I'm qualified for, if you'll permit it."

Another yelp sounded, and a door in the room directly behind Clem jerked open. Another man stood there, hair mussed.

"Clem! Is that Van back with the doctor?"

Clem glared at Rebekah again, his face granite.

"Yeah, Woodrow. It is."

Once she crossed the threshold into the ranch house, Rebekah blocked out Clem's drunken fury, Van's unsteadiness, and Woodrow's shocked expression and focused on getting into the room with the injured man as quickly as possible.

It turned out to be a bedroom that had once seen a woman's touch. Blue floral damask wallpaper was peeling, and there was a rip in the solid blue curtains. A red velvet wingback chair sat next to a full-size bed situated in the middle of the back wall.

A young man lay on his side, his back arched, face whiter than the pillow beneath his head. It looked as though the sheets hadn't been washed for some time, either.

Rebekah went to the bedside and noted the nightstand with an uncorked whiskey bottle and shot glass. She knocked the shot glass onto the floor, causing a clattering sound through the room amidst the cries of the young man. She set her medical bag on the table and began rolling up the sleeves of her robe.

Gaze still on her new patient, she asked, "What's his name?"

While Clem, Van, and Jimmy stayed close to the door, Woodrow came around the other side of the bed.

"Kurt." His voice sounded strained and tired.

Rebekah put her hand on the young man's shoulder and squeezed gently. "Kurt, I'm Doc Beck. I'm here to help."

He let out a long sigh. Rebekah ran her hands along his spine, pressing once. He jerked away, squeezing his eyes shut. She put a soft hand on his shoulder and glanced up at Woodrow. "What happened?"

Clem took two long strides into the room and gripped the frame at the end of the bed, shaking it. "Don't matter, lady. You just fix him up, and right now."

It wasn't the first time she'd heard this kind of demand. These men were doing something wrong when the injury occurred. Judging from the rips in Kurt's clothing and the gray dust, she guessed it was from being dragged by a horse. Or falling off a cliff. She would probably never know the whole story. Getting Kurt to a place where he was out of pain and on the way to healing was her primary goal.

Rebekah turned to her bag and pulled out a packet of the newly formulated aspirin. She squared herself with Clem as he stayed hunched over the bed frame, watching her.

"What has to be done will take a steady hand, something none of you seem to possess. Please leave." She nodded at Jimmy. "Except him. I need him to hold the lamp close."

Clem didn't break eye contact, leaning in as though to intimidate her by sheer force of will.

Rebekah held his gaze. "Please leave."

From the corner of her eye, she saw Woodrow clench and unclench his fists. But he said nothing. Rebekah was sure Clem flicked a glance at him, then said to her, "All right, lady doctor. You just see to it my brother walks out of here."

Clem released the frame with a shove, shaking the bed as he stepped back. He jerked his head at Van and Woodrow, gave Jimmy a stern look, and exited.

Once the three were out, Rebekah nodded at the door, telling Jimmy, "Close it."

CHAPTER 3

Rebekah had seen this sort of injury before. It crippled many cowboys for life, and it could very well do the same with this young man. Under normal circumstances, there would be very little she could do other than recommend he be taken to a hospital back east at the cost of thousands of dollars for specialty treatments and surgeries.

She highly doubted the oldest Baxter brother, Clem, was interested in hearing about it in the middle of the night out in the Texas Panhandle. She did have another solution. It was risky and experimental, and there were those with far more knowledge and experience than she had, but they weren't around. It wasn't something she could talk to Clem about. That left her with getting the patient's permission before proceeding.

Since she said she needed the boy, Jimmy, to stay in there with her, she put him to use. "Take that lamp off the wall and bring it over here, please. I need better light."

While Jimmy complied, she leaned over Kurt and gripped him by the shoulder again. He moaned, and her heart ached with its usual compassion at seeing someone in pain.

"Kurt, your back is severely out of alignment. I know maneuvers that could straighten it out. It's risky, but there's no other way I can get you out of pain and walking again. Do you want me to try?"

Kurt cracked his eyes open just a touch to reveal the same brown color as his brothers, and red. Not from tears. They'd given him too much whiskey.

His eyes darted around. Jimmy leaned over him with the lamp, and Kurt spotted him. He stammered, "Where...where's Clem?"

"He's right outside," Rebekah answered. "He told me to get you well. I'm going to do the very best I can. All right with you?"

Kurt closed his eyes again and gave a short nod. "Whatever Clem says."

Rebekah took a deep breath and motioned at Jimmy. "Now hold that lamp up just above him so that I can see his entire body."

Rebekah carefully rolled Kurt onto his stomach. She'd practiced a chiropractic adjustment with the doctor who had studied the science behind it, and though she wasn't an expert, she was confident enough in her knowledge of the human body to do maneuvers to realign Kurt's spine.

She started with a massage, feeling a popped-out vertebra. She crossed her hands over one another, took a breath, and push down quickly. A pop sounded, and Jimmy mumbled, "Ouch."

After massaging another one back into place, Rebekah noted Kurt was breathing easier and his body finally relaxed. She rolled him flat on his back and cleaned cuts and bruises on his face.

"You should be able to walk in a few days," she told him. Unfortunately, she wouldn't be around to see Kurt get out of that bed. She had a train to catch in the afternoon.

Jimmy looked relieved when she told him he could set the lamp back on the wall. He gave a little whistle. "You sure did a good job, ma'am. Just like a regular doctor."

Rebekah chuckled. People had said worse things about her as a female physician. "You are a flatterer, young man."

She glanced toward the closed door, knowing the Baxter boys would want word about their brother, but she was going to take these precious few moments to do what she had intended when she retained Jimmy. He was different from the Baxters, and she wanted to know how deep his loyalty ran in case she needed it.

The Baxters were a tough lot, especially Clem and Van, but she didn't fear them. Few things frightened her. Her mind was simply on leaving this place as soon as she could to get on with her mission. This boy might help with that.

She moved her bag to the dresser close to Jimmy and took her time recapping the alcohol bottle she'd used to clean the cuts.

Rebekah chose her words carefully. "How did a nice young man like you end up with the Baxters?"

Jimmy peeked into her bag, curious, and shrugged.

"Honestly, ma'am, I'd planned to leave the ranch sometime ago. But I had this nagging feeling that God wanted me to stay. Now I know why." He looked at her with a smile as though she should understand.

Rebekah cocked her head. "Why is that?"

"He wanted me here to help you."

Rebekah started to chuckle, but the seriousness of Jimmy's face held her in check. He took his faith to heart, a rarity in this sort of setting. She didn't want to mock it, even if she no longer shared it.

"I see. You've been a valuable help, Mr. Jimmy."

He gave her a wide grin. "Thank you, Doc Beck...What did you say your name was?"

"Doctor Rebekah LaRoche."

"La what?"

"I'm part French."

"You don't sound French, ma'am."

"Parlez-vous français?"

He gulped. "I'll stick with calling you Doc Beck."

She put the bottle in her bag and patted his arm. "Miss Rebekah will suffice."

"You speaking French again?"

Rebekah chuckled. Jimmy was intelligent, if not well educated. "'Suffice' does have its roots in Old French, but it's purely English. It means calling me Miss Rebekah is just fine."

She headed for the door. "It's time to tell Mr. Baxter that his brother will sleep well tonight."

In the sitting room that she originally came through to the bedroom, the three Baxter brothers came to their feet. Woodrow asked, "Kurt going to be all right?"

Rebekah nodded. "Everything went well, but he should remain in bed for the next two days. Please see that he doesn't move around. I'll keep watch over him tonight, and then I must leave in the morning. I have a train to catch in Amarillo. Goodnight."

Rebekah went back into the bedroom, dismissed Jimmy, and curled herself up to sleep in the red velvet wingback chair next to the bed. She'd slept in worse conditions before.

CHAPTER 4

Before dawn, Rebekah was awakened by the bedroom door opening. She jerked and watched Clem Baxter bend over his sleeping brother in the darkness, a stream of light coming in from the lamp in the sitting room.

"He doing all right?" Clem asked.

He looked haggard. Rebekah wasn't sure if he was hungover or had continued drinking all night. Either way, she didn't want him disturbing her patient.

Rebekah held in a stretch, remaining in the chair, hoping he would quietly leave. She said softly, "He slept fine, but he needs more rest."

Thankfully, Clem left with little noise, leaving the door open. Rebekah caught the smell of bacon sizzling on a stove. But she didn't care to take breakfast with these men nor wait for daylight to leave.

She stood, stretched, and shook out her robe still secured over her nightgown. She checked on her patient, who was sleeping soundly, then repacked her medical bag and snapped it closed, catching sight of herself in the mirror over the vanity by the wall.

What a fright. Her long, sable brown hair was a tangled mess from the night ride, her eyes swollen from lack of sleep. She had her father's eyes, brown with a hint of gold. Her skin was the same shade as his, leading Clem to mistake her for Mexican until he looked close.

Rebekah quickly did what she could to her hair, knowing it would be wrecked again on the ride back into Amarillo, especially if she were transported the same way she got there. She checked her pocket watch. 5 a.m.

There was little hope of reaching the Garland home before dawn. She resigned herself to being gawked at when arriving in town in her nightgown and robe. At least she was leaving Amarillo and wouldn't return unless her sponsor sent her there.

But he had sent her on another mission, and it was time she got to it.

Rebekah picked up her heavy bag and went into the sitting room. To the right was an alcove with a kitchen and long table where the Baxter boys were gathered around with platters of bacon and biscuits. It looked like Woodrow was the cook. He shoveled scrambled eggs from the skillet onto plates in front of Van and Clem.

Woodrow, tall and lean, glanced up and nodded at her. "Clem says Kurt is going to be all right."

Rebekah stifled another yawn. "He does need to stay in bed and should be seen by another doctor in two days. But yes, I believe he will make a full recovery."

Woodrow motioned with the skillet toward an empty chair at the table. "Sit down and have a bite, Doc."

"I would prefer to go back to town now. I can take breakfast there and sleep until my train. Do you have a buggy or wagon that Jimmy could take me there in?"

Van started shoveling the hearty breakfast in, but Clem sat hunch over his plate, staring at it. He said, "You're staying here until my brother gets out of that bed."

Rebekah kept her expression neutral, not entirely surprised by the cold words. Still, her stomach tightened. "As much as I wish that were possible, Mr. Baxter, I have a train to catch. My services are needed in Zapata, New Mexico Territory, and I must leave on this afternoon's train."

Clem rose from his chair, giving his plate of bacon and eggs a shove. Woodrow halted by the stove, iron skillet still in hand as he looked between his brother and Rebekah.

Clem spoke slowly, accentuating his long draw. "I said you're staying here, lady. And what I say goes in this house."

Rebekah weighed her options. Would he physically force her to stay if she walked out the door? The look in his eyes gave her the answer.

Woodrow shifted, putting him a foot closer to his brother, skillet in his right hand and held a little higher.

"Clem, you can't keep this woman here against her will. If she wants to leave—"

Clem turned on his brother, drawing his six-gun and cocking it. Van halted, fork midway to his mouth. Woodrow didn't move, and Rebekah recognized an intense battle in his eyes. She held her breath.

Woodrow glanced at her, then back at Clem before taking a slow step back to the stove and settling the skillet on it. He stared at it as Clem said, "Don't you ever do that again, Woodrow Baxter."

Rebekah backed toward the bedroom door, keeping her movements even. Clem jerked his head to glare at her, gun still out. He was hungover, but she had a feeling he could shoot what he aimed at.

She stepped carefully across the threshold, not looking at it. Clem barked, "Van, keep an eye on her. Don't let her go anywhere without you knowing."

There was no argument, and moments later, Van appeared in the doorway with his plate of bacon and eggs, giving her a look that said he blamed her for interrupting his hot breakfast.

Rebekah turned back to the bed where Kurt was still asleep, oblivious to his brothers' conflict. Just as well. Rebekah felt Kurt was a sensitive soul, dying to please his brothers. She wondered how he survived in a family like this.

❦

AFTER THE CONFRONTATION AT BREAKFAST, Rebekah had dozed off again in the wing-back chair. The room was lit with dawn when approaching steps alerted her that someone was coming.

Jimmy came through the door, arms and hands full as he side-stepped Van, who didn't stir from where he'd dozed off in a chair he dragged in from the sitting room. Kurt was still asleep.

Rebekah scrambled to her feet, blinking as Jimmy approached without his grin. He must have heard what happened with Clem and Woodrow, but he made an effort to sound cheerful as he held up his load.

"Thought you might want some breakfast, ma'am, and fresh clothes."

In his arms was a bundle of clothes and in his hands, he balanced a plate of bacon and biscuits and a tin cup of coffee.

Rebekah quickly took the food and cup before he made a mess. "You're very kind, Mr. Jimmy."

"Oh, no ma'am, no mister to it, it's just Jimmy."

"Well, Just Jimmy. Thank you."

He grinned. "I like that, Doc. I want to be known as a fair and just man."

"A fine ambition." Unfortunately, he wouldn't see it modeled on the Baxter Ranch.

When Jimmy left, Rebekah used the closet to change into the men's clothing. The closet was larger than she thought it would be and over half empty. No women's clothes, only two pairs of trousers and three shirts hung on hooks along with a musty brown coat.

Rebekah slipped out of her robe and nightgown to pull on the clean white shirt that looked about Jimmy's size, along with a pair of his trousers. He must only have possessed one belt because her outfit included a short rope to hold the tan trousers up. She hardly needed it. Jimmy was as slender as she was. It was wholly improper for her to wear trousers, and she felt ridiculous, but they were practical.

The afternoon passed slowly. Kurt woke but said little, his expression miserable. Rebekah had a feeling it wasn't from pain, especially since she gave him more aspirin. Likely, he feared the coming displeasure of his brother for doing whatever he'd done that caused his injury.

Van moved into the sitting room, though he ordered her to stay in his line of sight at all times. That limited Rebekah to moving between checking on her patient and the wing back chair. She insisted on going to the outhouse without accompaniment, to Van's grumbling.

On her short trip to the outhouse, Rebekah took in the dusty but fresh air of the open country. Milkweed grew wild in the yard between the house and the large barn and corral. Chickens clucked, pecking and scratching a meal from the dry earth and vegetation. Open country surrounded the place, not a tree in sight—only the road leading up to the house.

Three ranch hands were working colts in the corral. They paused to watch her and then went on with their business. No one seemed happy at the Baxter Ranch.

They did have fine-looking horses. Any one of them could easily carry Rebekah back to Amarillo if she felt threatened enough to risk it. Clem might start drinking again anytime, and her train wasn't important enough to test his temper today.

Still, in this situation, she felt it was wise to assert as much control as she could, at least with Van, the youngest Baxter. She couldn't push it too much because he was feeling his power and control with the second oldest son at odds with the oldest. Family dynamics could be so complicated.

Rebekah was determined to understand them as much as possible in order to get out of there unscathed. Her journey to New Mexico Territory would be delayed yet a few more days. Doctor McKinnon, her sponsor, would be worried when she didn't arrive and received no response to his telegrams that he would send to Amarillo tomorrow.

Returning to the room, she found Kurt awake and vomiting. Not only was he injured, but his foolish brothers were to thank for his hangover.

She cleaned the mess and propped Kurt up enough to help him drink the coffee Woodrow made before the noon meal. Kurt, eyes glassy and red but clearing, looked up at Rebekah like he wanted to say something, wanted to ask her a question, but he held it in and sipped the coffee. She changed the bandages on his cuts and helped him find a position to lay in that would keep him straight as he rested.

The afternoon ticked away slowly. Rebekah settled in with a book of poetry she had in her bag. She paused and pulled out her pocket watch to see it was 3:15 p.m.

If the train were on time, it would be leaving the depot at Amarillo about now. The ticket in her reticule back at the Garland home was worthless.

CHAPTER 5

Jimmy spent most of the day working in the barn. He was supposed to be riding fence, but Clem Baxter wanted the ranch hands close. He didn't say why, but Jimmy heard gossip among the hands that the Baxter brothers had blown up a chunk of rock in the Palo Duro Canyon in their war with the Lowells.

Jimmy wasn't surprised they'd caused a rockslide, but he wasn't happy about it either. If it hadn't been for Doc Beck, he would draw his pay and ride out. But as it was, he was grateful for the order to stay close and had swapped duties of mending corrals in the pasture on the backside of the house to working in the barn, oiling saddles. That kept him closer to the house in case the lady doctor needed him.

He was the only one on the ranch that would stick up for Miss Rebekah. Woodrow was too intimidated by his brother. That could change someday if Clem pushed hard enough. Jimmy had seen it in Woodrow's eyes.

Not that Jimmy had much experience reading people at his sixteen years of age. But he had enough to know when a showdown was coming.

He hefted the saddle he had been working on and carried it into the tack room located inside the barn, settling it on a saddle rack. When the jingle of the stirrups stopped, he heard other sounds coming into the barn.

Be still.

Jimmy had heard that quiet voice in his spirit before, and things always turned out better when he listened. He held his breath and heard someone coming into the barn.

"Take the palomino." It was Clem. "She's got stout legs for the canyon. Don't get too close to the Lowell place. You take a look, see what they're up to, and get right back here. I want you watching the woman most of the time. Can't trust Woodrow to do it right."

"What about that doc anyway?" Van's voice. "Folks from town will be wondering where she is. Won't that bring the law?"

There was a long pause before Clem spoke again. "The law is the reason I'm keeping her. The Lowells went straight to the sheriff in Canyon City after last night. One of their men got killed in the slide. The sheriff'll be out here, and the best thing we can have is a little leverage. That's why I'm keeping her around."

"Even after Kurt gets better?"

"Kurt don't need her to get better. He's a Baxter."

Their voices were getting louder. They were coming into the tack room.

Jimmy darted into a back corner where two saddle racks easily concealed his bony frame. He squatted behind them just as Clem and Van entered. There was an edge in Clem's voice that Jimmy hadn't heard before. If he didn't know better, he'd wonder if Clem was scared. Of what?

Their father had had such a fearless, iron fist on them. He even whacked Jimmy for saying maybe the Baxters should leave the Lowells in peace, and said he'd shoot Jimmy if he ever questioned him again. That was when Jimmy nearly left but felt the good Lord wanted him to stay.

Clem was like his father, but without as many years experience at being mean without losing control of his boys.

Van lifted one of the newly oiled saddles off the rack and turned to his brother. "I'm with you all the way, Clem. You know that."

"I wouldn't have it any other way."

Coming from a different man, that might sound like a compliment. Coming from Clem Baxter, it was a threat, like his father always did. Jimmy recognized Clem's temper getting shorter and shorter, and there was no saying what he might do if he got cornered.

CHAPTER 6

Toward suppertime, Rebekah wasn't sure whether she should ask the brothers to bring her a cot to sleep in the room with Kurt or settle into the chair again. She was getting tired of that chair but lying on a bed felt too vulnerable. She wanted to be ready to run. Being dressed in men's clothes would help.

But she was going stir crazy in the bedroom. She tended Kurt, which wasn't much other than helping him eat and stay comfortable. He didn't respond to her attempts to engage him in conversation, so she settled for reading aloud in the awkward silence. But she'd finished the book before evening and felt exhausted. Her lack of sleep and comfort wasn't helping her temperament.

When Woodrow changed out guard duties with Van, she snapped at the youngest Baxter boy. "If you expect me to stay caged on this ranch another minute, I need something sensible to read."

Woodrow glanced at her on his way out but kept moving as he said, "Supper'll be ready soon."

Rebekah crossed her arms and stared at Van, the one who had

31

yanked her from the Garland home and dragged her to this ranch on the edge of the Palo Duro Canyon.

"Well?"

"Well, what? You think we got time for reading on this ranch?"

"You would do well to engage in civilized activities rather than whatever caused your brother's injury."

Van's nostrils flared. She'd struck a nerve, one she might regret.

Kurt shifted on the bed, the whites of his eyes showing his fear. He was fully sober and awake now.

"It wasn't Van's fault, honest, ma'am. He couldn't help that I slipped off the ledge when I tried to pull him up. I'm plain clumsy, ma'am. Clumsy and no good to Clem or anyone."

Rebekah kept her gaze locked on Van. "I see. Was Clem the cause of all of this, or was it something that sprang from your imagination, Van? Reading would serve you well. Then maybe you could concoct a scheme that didn't injure your brothers."

Van matched her stare. "You need to learn how to talk to your betters."

He advanced toward her, eyes blazing. She'd pushed him too hard. Her mind went to her medical bag on the table by the bed.

"You're not leaving this ranch, lady."

She lunged for her bag, but Van grabbed her by the arm and jerked her around. He shoved her into the wall, pressing one arm across her throat and cutting off her air.

"Not ever!"

"Van!" Kurt struggled to sit up.

The black dots clouding her vision made Rebekah raise her knee quick and land it right where she needed to. Van yelled and loosened enough for her to shove him away. She caught her breath and reached for her bag, but his fingers sank into her hair and yanked her head back.

"You're going to regret that, lady."

"Let her go!" It was Jimmy.

Van shoved Rebekah to the floor. She rolled and looked up in time to see Jimmy plow into Van headfirst, catching Van in the gut.

They crashed into the red velvet wing-back chair, breaking the back legs. Van rolled clear and whipped out his pistol. He swung it at Jimmy's head, but Jimmy dodged it and bit down on Van's wrist. Van howled.

A shout came from the doorway as Woodrow rushed in. "What's going on—"

The gun went off. The bullet struck Woodrow.

CHAPTER 7

The echo of gunfire was the only sound in the room. When it died, no one moved. Rebekah stayed frozen near the wall, not wanting to move for fear of Van jerking the trigger again.

Then Van shoved away from Jimmy and approached his brother sprawled on the floor. Van still held his six-gun, his hand shaking.

Jimmy got to his feet and helped Rebekah up, looking her over for injuries. She stepped around him with a pat on his arm to let him know she was all right, and started toward Woodrow. But she halted at the sight of Clem in the doorway.

She met his cold gaze then went forward to kneel beside Woodrow Baxter. He was clenching his bleeding right shoulder.

A quick examination showed the bullet had passed through. Rebekah spoke quietly to him.

"I'll need to clean and stitch this."

Woodrow groaned and pushed himself to a sitting position, struggling to his feet. Rebekah helped him since neither of his brothers moved. Woodrow hadn't said a word to her when he was guarding her earlier. She knew he was too much under Clem's control to help her escape.

Now there was a fire in his eyes. Once on his feet, Woodrow staggered a step, then glared at Clem.

"This what you want for our family? Blasting us all to pieces, same as Pa?"

Van shoved his revolver back in his holster. "Don't be saying anything against Pa or Clem, neither."

The swagger was gone from his voice, replaced by an uncertain gruffness. Woodrow rounded on him, hand still clutched over his bleeding shoulder.

"That all you got to say for yourself after shooting your brother?"

Rebekah didn't know what would happen if the sharp words continued, so she took over the situation. She grabbed Woodrow by the arm and guided him toward the door.

"Let's get you fixed up. Jimmy, please bring my bag."

She halted at the doorway because Clem still filled it, not moving as he watched them with sullen eyes. His gaze flicked to the blood soaking his brother's gray shirt.

He finally stepped aside. Woodrow stumbled through, Rebekah's firm grip on his arm keeping him from falling to the floor. They went to the room one door down, Jimmy close behind with her medical bag.

Good Jimmy. That's a good boy.

THE LOW RUMBLE in the distance warned Rebekah of the approaching thunderstorm. She wasn't sure how common spring tornadoes were in this part of Texas, if they were as bad as Indian Territory which she had left before coming to Amarillo on her way to Zapata, New Mexico Territory. But it didn't matter.

Dodging tornadoes was less risky than remaining another night in this house under the thumb of Clem Baxter.

After patching Woodrow's flesh wound and settling him in the lower bunk in the small bedroom—Woodrow muttering something about how Kurt should be in the top bunk—Rebekah set about quietly repacking her bag.

She had retained Jimmy on the excuse of needing his assistance when Clem ordered him out of the house. It was the last battle she needed to win with Clem Baxter. She knew which direction Canyon City was, but navigating her way there in the dark alone was not appealing. Besides, Jimmy had risked his life to help her, and she wouldn't leave him behind in this volatile situation.

"Cork and hand me that bottle, please." Rebekah nodded at the brown bottle by the bedside as she settled her instruments back in the bag, everything arranged neatly. Keeping items organized in her bag helped keep her mind organized and calm as she prepared to take a risk.

Jimmy complied. When he was close, she whispered, "I'm leaving tonight. Do you want to go with me?"

Jimmy jerked his head up as though surprised at her words or perhaps the conspiratorial tone of her voice. He didn't seem surprised that she trusted him, nor should he. He had proven himself that day.

Jimmy glanced over at Woodrow, who had drifted off to sleep with a bit of help from Rebekah. It would be better if he was in a deep sleep and not incur Clem's wrath when she disappeared. And the rest would help him recover from the wound quicker. He was the only one who had a chance of actually running this ranch without running it off the rails.

Dipping his head and speaking in the same low tone, Jimmy's boyish voice squeaked when he said, "I'll help you escape, Miss Rebekah. I know the way."

Those were the words Rebekah had wanted to hear from the

moment she realized Clem Baxter was a force to be reckoned with. It was why she had retained Jimmy the first night to help with Kurt and had watched him carefully. They could help each other now.

Rebekah strapped her bag closed with a nonchalant glance over her shoulder, out the open door. Clem and Van were seated in the sitting room, staring at the blazing fireplace that made the whole house too hot. They both held shot glasses of whiskey.

She finished closing her bag and spoke to Jimmy. "Please go to the barn and have a couple of horses saddled for us at 10 p.m. I have a plan for getting me out of the house. I need you to have a plan to get us off this ranch."

"You can count on me, Doc."

"I am counting on you, just Jimmy."

<hr />

IT WASN'T hard to mix a sleeping powder into Van's coffee when he took up guard duty between the two doors of where Kurt and Woodrow rested. Clem had retired in his own bedroom, telling Van he would spell him after a while. Rebekah had gotten herself a coffee and one for Van as a sort of peace offering. He didn't thank her, but at least he wasn't shoving her into the wall and choking her.

She entered the bedroom with Kurt. To her dismay, he was wide awake and wanting to talk.

Rebekah settled herself in the chair Van had brought from the sitting room. There was satisfaction in that dreadful wing-back chair getting broken.

Kurt rolled his face toward her. "Ma'am, we weren't always this bad. Wasn't till Ma died. This was her and Pa's room. Now since Pa died, we don't use it for nothing. It hurts being in here."

Rebekah nodded, fingering her watch in her trouser pocket.

She had timed things for Van to doze off shortly. She and Jimmy needed as much of a head start on Clem as they could get.

But Kurt kept talking.

"I didn't want to do it, didn't want to blow up the canyon and kill the Lowell's sheep. I don't think Woodrow did either, but Clem's been acting so much like Pa that we all do whatever he says. Is that wrong, ma'am? To stick with your flesh and blood like that?"

Rebekah's mind turned to what was once home for her. "I was fortunate to grow up in a fine family with a father who taught me to stand up for myself but to seek justice and mercy whenever I could."

Kurt swallowed. "He sounds like a good man."

"He was."

Kurt blinked, and a tear rolled down his cheek. Rebekah wished she could take him with her. But she learned long ago she couldn't adopt every stray she came across. Only some. Getting out of there and sending the law back to the Baxter Ranch was the best thing she could do for this young man.

Rebekah leaned forward and squeezed Kurt's wrist. "Rest now. By tomorrow, you should be able to get out of bed and move around a little. But no riding for at least two weeks. Do you understand?"

She wished she could be sure he would follow her directions, but that was a problem she faced with all of her patients. Kurt nodded, and there was a sincerity in his eyes that told her he would at least try. If Clem didn't get in the way.

Rebekah leaned back in the chair, and he took that as the end of the conversation and closed his eyes. But he didn't go to sleep right away and Rebekah stayed tense. She stared out the window of the bedroom, a clear view of the barn. No lantern light showed there. The ranch hands had retired for the night.

What of Jimmy? Could he saddle horses in the dark? Her neck ached from the strain of watching.

After several minutes, she eased to her feet and glanced through the open doorway. Van was nodding off, but he still held the coffee cup. If he dropped it when he fell asleep, the racket would bring Clem out and railing at him. Rebekah needed to time it right to slip out, get the cup, and hope Van didn't fall out of the chair. It was a risk she would have to take. Fortunately, the back door was on the opposite side of Clem's bedroom, and the thunder kept rumbling closer.

She didn't know the sound could be heard for so long before the storm actually arrived.

CHAPTER 8

R ebekah managed to catch the cup when it slipped from Van's hand. She quietly set it on the floor. The storm finally arrived, pouring sheets on the tin roof of the ranch house. It was deafening and wouldn't be at all pleasant to ride in, but the noise would help cover her exit, not to mention the tracks.

She quietly pulled on the large brown coat from the closet and picked up her medical bag from the floor beside Kurt. With one last sorrowful look at the young man, she headed for the back door.

She turned the knob and the door flew toward her face. She braced her palm against it, wincing at the storm's sounds rushing in. She glanced back to see Van shift in his chair, but he was still in a deep sleep. Was Clem?

She slipped around the door and pulled it closed firmly against the wind. The wind! It pressed her against the outside wall of the house, and the rain stung her eyes. She blinked several times to clear her vision. The yard was so dark and the rain so thick it took her several moments to get a clear line on the barn.

When she did, she ran for it, mud sucking at the oversized

boots Jimmy had given her to go with her man-outfit. She wondered if she should shuck the boots and go barefoot, but the area's rocky terrain warned that her tender feet needed protection. It'd been a long time since she had run barefoot.

Rebekah started to open the smaller door leading into the barn when she heard a hiss that was anything but subtle.

"Doc Beck! Over here."

Rebekah glanced to the corral at her left and saw Jimmy beckoning wildly at her. She ducked between the slats of the corral, again grateful for the trousers. But when Jimmy grabbed her shoulders and tried to help her through, she almost fell.

Straightening, she said, "I appreciate help, Jimmy, but please wait until I ask for it."

He didn't seem to hear her as he darted under the overhang in the corral where two horses were tied. He tossed her a rain slicker like the one he wore. She slipped into it and grabbed the reins of the horse he indicated, but he held the horse fast and squinted at her in the dark, water dribbling off his tan Stetson. He looked deadly serious.

"Only one of these horses and gear belongs to me. Is it stealing if we take the other one and turn it loose later? It'll find its way back to the ranch here."

"Considering that I am being held here against my will, I have no qualms about borrowing this horse without asking."

Jimmy looked more relieved than she expected. "Good. I ain't never stolen anything in my life."

Rebekah smiled. "I believe you."

She mounted as Jimmy led his horse to the far end of the corral.

He unlatched the gate just as a tremendous boom rattled Rebekah in the saddle. Her horse shied and reared back, doing a quick paw at the air before settling on all fours again. Rebekah held her balance and glanced at the splintered wood of the corral gate. It wasn't thunder she'd heard.

She looked over her shoulder to see Clem Baxter standing on the back porch, double-barrel shotgun aimed at them. He had another slug left.

"Look out, Jimmy!"

Jimmy slapped her horse's rump, sending it flying through the open gate while he swung aboard his horse. The second blast sounded somewhere behind her.

Rebekah grasped for a solid hold to keep her in the saddle as the horse galloped at full speed, her medical bag banging the saddle where she had tied it to the horn.

They plunged into the darkness. Rebekah could barely discern the road as she gripped the saddle horn and glanced back to see Jimmy chasing after her, full tilt.

They had made it. At least, for the moment.

Jimmy waved wildly at her, and she tightened her grip on the reins enough to bring her horse to a resistant trot. Jimmy swung up beside her, bringing his arm around in a sweeping motion.

"This way!"

He darted off the road in between an abundance of mesquite trees. Rebekah turned her horse in a circle and bolted after Jimmy. They were going the wrong way for either Canyon City or Amarillo, but she trusted Jimmy and his instincts. She had little choice.

They rode awhile before Jimmy finally slowed. The rain had as well, although they were leaving a trail a blind man could follow.

Rebekah halted next to Jimmy. He was breathing hard. She looked back in the general direction of the Baxter place.

"I owe you a great deal of thanks, just Jimmy. But why are we going in the opposite direction of Amarillo?"

Jimmy nodded in front of them. "That's why."

Rebekah peered ahead at a gaping black hole. She couldn't distinguish where the land and sky parted. She sat very still and allowed her eyes to adjust. Then a flash of lightning from the roiling storm light up the spectacle of buttes, mesas, and cliffs.

They were at the Palo Duro Canyon.

Jimmy said, "When I seen Clem ready to come after us, I knew we wouldn't have enough of a head start. That man is a hard rider. But the canyon's got more hiding places than a dog has fleas."

"Your vernacular is astonishing, Jimmy."

He looked at her, the whites of his eyes gleaming in the darkness.

"You speaking French again, ma'am?"

Rebekah smiled and shook her head, nudging her horse forward to the rim. Jimmy pushed his horse up in front of her, halting them both.

"Best let me go first, Miss Rebekah. One wrong step, and it'll be a faster trip to the bottom than a lady should make."

It took half an hour of concentration to maneuver her mount along what Jimmy had coined a trail down the side of the canyon. She never saw evidence of one during the occasional flashes of lightning. The rough terrain was unforgiving on them and the horses. The entire time, she was listening for the sound of Clem Baxter's booming gun.

She had to give Jimmy credit for his smart move. By the time Clem could alert Van and mount, it was too late for him to see where Jimmy and Rebekah veered off the road. He would think they headed straight into Amarillo or Canyon City, and there was a good chance a young boy and a rusty woman rider would've been caught in the open.

She did hope Jimmy had a plan for getting them out of the canyon and to law enforcement. Rebekah had to trust Jimmy, even in the next steps she guided her horse in.

When they reached the bottom, the clouds parted to let the half-moon shine down on the floor. It was so sudden, so unexpected, Rebekah caught her breath at the shimmering light bathing the rock walls of the Palo Duro. It was unearthly, as though they had stepped into a reality previously beyond comprehension. The magnitude of the walls and the dome of the sky above them were breathtaking.

"You all right, Miss Rebekah?"

Rebekah brought her gaze down to realize she had halted her horse, and Jimmy was several feet in front of her, turned in his saddle.

She nodded. "Let's keep going."

They maneuvered to the canyon's gravel and rock floor to a deep creek bed that cut through the area, carving it out like an arroyo. The horses splashed through and picked up a fast pace to climb the other side between the rocks. Jimmy halted with a glance back to check on her. It was justified. Rebekah was so tired, she feared falling from the saddle.

She observed how the terrain leveled before the next climb up the creek bed wall. "We should rest here. The pinnacle will block us from sight if Clem decides to come to the canyon."

Jimmy looked around. "I don't know if that's a good idea, Miss Rebekah."

"My joints say it is a wonderful idea." She swung down from the saddle and took a shaky breath. Her body trembled with fatigue and the hard ride. The thought of a few hours of sleep did sound wondrous.

"Yes, ma'am." Jimmy mimicked her in dismounting. "And I don't think Clem will come this way. We'll ride out tomorrow and on over to Canyon City. I have friends there, and we'll tell the sheriff what Clem did."

Rebekah unhooked her medical bag, set it aside, and started to unsaddle the horse.

"Oh, no, ma'am!"

Jimmy rushed over, causing her horse to toss his head in annoyance. Rebekah raised an eyebrow at her young companion.

"It's better if the horses are allowed to rest without this burden on them," she said.

"Yes ma'am, but I'll take care of it. You go on and find yourself a place to bed down."

Jimmy was sweet in his innocent, whole-hearted effort to be a gentleman. He would grow into a fine young man someday, with a little help.

"Very well, just Jimmy. I assume we shouldn't build a fire to dry out by?"

"No, ma'am. But you can have my coat. It'll keep you warm."

He started to take off his slicker, but Rebekah waved him off. "Mine will do."

She glanced back up the way they had come. The creek and a rock pinnacle stood sentry over their location.

Jimmy said, "I'll keep watch tonight, Doc. Don't you worry."

Rebekah nodded absently. She rarely worried. Her wits and good sense could get her out of most any situation.

CHAPTER 9

The train whistled loud as it roared toward the depot. It didn't slow despite the lone passenger waiting on the platform, waving fiercely at it. The train barreled forward. It suddenly jumped off the track and headed straight for the waving figure.

Rebekah screamed when she realized she was that figure.

She jerked up, her breathing coming in labored gasps. A dream. A bad dream. Or was it?

The roar was still coming toward her where she lay on the hard floor of the canyon. The horses bounced against their hobbles, eyes rolling in fright.

Rebekah scrambled to her feet, pushing against the rocks she had bedded down on. Somewhere above the roar, Jimmy shouted, "High ground! Get to high ground!"

She spotted Jimmy scrambling away from the creek and to the horses that he quickly unhobbled.

"Don't just stand there, Doc! Flash flood, get to higher ground!"

A train was indeed barreling toward them, somewhere out of sight. Rebekah ran for her medical bag that she had left close to

46

the horses. Jimmy met her, grabbing the bag and her arm as they bolted up the incline from the creek. The horses galloped away in a mad dash, running as hard as the humans, only faster.

Rebekah glanced behind her to glimpse a mighty river bursting out from around the corner of the pinnacle and engulf the creek bed as if it had been merely a drainage ditch. She looked forward, measuring the distance of the ground before them compared to the water's height. They wouldn't make it.

"Lord, help us," Jimmy whisper-gasped as the red water hit them from behind.

The incredible rush of limbs, leaves, and brush pushed Rebekah off her feet. She squeezed her eyes shut, waiting to be crushed into the rocks. But she wasn't.

Opening her eyes, she realized Jimmy had hooked his arm around her and was holding on for dear life as the water tried to pull them under. But what was holding him in place against the onslaught and keeping them from being swept away?

Rebekah clung to Jimmy, the only solid thing within her grasp. She kicked in the water, trying to find a solid foothold, but she couldn't. The strong current pulled at her waterlogged boots and sucked them off her feet.

All she could do was hold onto Jimmy and hope he could hold on as the river pulled hard.

It was over in seconds. As quickly as the rush of water filled that portion of the canyon, it began to recede. It still gushed like a river, but Jimmy and Rebekah were high enough on the wall to be away from the strongest current pull. But even as the water level dropped, Rebekah couldn't get her feet on under her. She was still being pulled downward by the current.

"You all right, ma'am?"

Rebekah took a shallow breath. It was hard to breathe with Jimmy's grip around her, holding her up.

"I'll let you know when my feet are on firm ground again."

"Can you climb up behind me?"

Rebekah twisted her gaze to look beyond Jimmy's shoulder. She realized his right arm was extended at a severe angle, his knuckles bloody and white as he clung to a mesquite tree on the wall that should have ripped out against the pressure.

"If you can keep hanging on to that for another minute, I can climb out of here."

"Be careful, ma'am."

The water level had dropped more, and Rebekah was able to get a bare toehold in the wall, twisting in Jimmy's grip that he barely loosened. She pushed herself up and used the rocks to work her way out of the water behind him. She heard his relieved moan when her body pressure was finally off him. She pushed until she found firm ground, then twisted and reached back.

"Now, give me your hand."

"I don't want to pull you back down here, ma'am."

"You do as I say, young man."

"Yes ma'am."

Jimmy shifted so that he could reach higher with his free hand. She could see the intense pain on his face caused by the angle of his shoulder. She wasn't sure from this position, but it didn't appear dislocated.

Another miracle. Maybe she should consider believing in those again and pride herself a little less on her own wits.

CHAPTER 10

Jimmy collapsed on the rocky slope beside Rebekah, breathing hard. His breathing turned to a chuckle, then laughter. Rebekah joined him and sat up before she choked.

"Well, just Jimmy. You're a good partner. Next time, I'll let you pick the camping spot."

Jimmy wiped water out of his eyes and winced. Rebekah immediately probed his shoulder, making him yelp and draw away. She grabbed him by his purple bandana and held him still while she felt for damage.

"You'll be sore a few days, but you'll live." Then she asked, "Do you know what happened to my bag?"

"I threw it to higher ground. I think."

They spent the next several minutes searching the rocks, being careful not to lose footing and slide back into the impromptu river that continued to recede.

"Here it is! Or what's left of it."

Rebekah groaned as Jimmy fished the bag out of a puddle of water and held it open. One of the straps was broken, and it looked like most of her implements and medicines were gone.

Rebekah started to take it from him, but he gave it another

shake. "Still awful heavy for all the stuff being gone." He poked his nose into the bag, but she could see his grin. "Say, you have a false bottom in this."

He pried it open and gave a low whistle. "If them Baxter boys catch up with us, they'll be the ones hollering for help."

Rebekah sighed and took the bag. "It is not polite to rummage through a lady's bag, Jimmy."

He looked truly shamed, and she regretted how the words had come out harsh. She patted his arm. "I'm sorry. I do get cranky when I'm jolted out of bed abruptly."

He grinned. "That's all right, Doc."

They searched for Rebekah's boots, but she knew they would be at the bottom of the flooded creek. She shrugged. "I'm afraid they're gone. We have to move on."

Jimmy lifted one foot and started yanking his boot off, hopping around. "You can wear mine, Doc. Can't have you getting your feet cut up."

He gave a hard yank, and his foot came free right as he landed on his backside with a thump.

Rebekah chuckled. "You keep them, Jimmy. I'll be able to navigate barefoot."

"I know a place we can bed down. We just gotta climb up Brushy Butte. Follow me."

Lit by the half-moon, Jimmy led the way up what might have been an actual trail shown by how it was deeply rutted. Probably an old game trail used for years by Comanches riding their horses down to water. There was ancient history in this canyon, but at the moment, Rebekah was interested in simply surviving it.

They climbed around a steep bend in the trail marked by an enormous prickly pear cactus, and Rebekah spotted a dugout set in a dip on the other side. It looked as though it hadn't been used in a few years, although maybe it had looked that way since the day it was built.

Jimmy beckoned for her to follow as they approached the

door that was cocked. Jimmy pushed it the rest of the way open. "Wait here. I'll check for rattlers."

Rebekah didn't object.

Jimmy set her bag on the porch and stepped inside. She heard him rustling around and, in a few moments, he had a lantern lit, its light shining through the open door.

He said, "All clear."

Rebekah took her bag inside, staring at the wood stove with longing. What she wouldn't do for a long hot bath and a clean morning dress.

Jimmy shook out a blanket, chewed on by moths, sending a puff of dust through the room and revealing a cot in even worse shape.

"All the comforts of home," he said.

"You must have grown up in a very strange home, Jimmy."

Jimmy looked at her with an odd expression, then grinned.

"Sure did. I was raised in the swamps of Florida, wrestling alligators and fighting Seminoles. I wanted to see the west, so I came on out to Texas."

Rebekah set her bag on the rickety table in the center of the room and gave him a sidelong look. Wherever did he get such a story?

"Jimmy, the Seminoles, along with the other Five Tribes of the Cherokee, Choctaw, Chickasaw, and Muskogee Creek, were forcibly removed from their homelands and to Indian Territory decades ago."

Jimmy rubbed his shoulder. "Oh. Well, must've been some mean city slickers then."

Rebekah shook her head and rummaged through a small chest by the door. No clean clothing, but the two woolen blankets stored in it were in better shape than the one that had been on the cot.

She took them to the wall furthest from the door. "I'll sleep on the floor here. You can have that flea trap if you want."

Jimmy perked up. "Really? You don't mind?"

"Absolutely not."

Rebekah spread one of the blankets on the floor away from the door, the other on top of it, making her bed. Jimmy rummaged through a corner cabinet.

"I take shelter here sometimes when chasing strays in the canyon," he said. "Left behind two cans of beans last time. Want one?"

"No, thank you."

Jimmy shrugged and began cutting open one can with his knife. "I've been wanting to ask, where are you from? You don't talk like anyone I've ever heard."

"I'm French. And Omaha."

"You're from Omaha?"

"That's...accurate."

Jimmy's innocence was fascinating. He seemed to know a little about many things but not a lot about the world. It was almost as though he'd learned what he did from books. That left him with an abundance of questions and ignorance of real people and cultures, like the Omahas. Perhaps his knowledge of Indians was limited to tall tales and outlandish dime novels. But there was a goodness to him that Rebekah admired. There was a chance she could help him along with the rest of life.

"Do all French people have dark skin like you?" he asked.

"The ones from the Omaha do."

"How come you're heading to New Mexico Territory?"

Rebekah settled on the floor, pulling one foot up to examine a cut. The sand she had walked over cleaned it well. "I was supposed to be there weeks ago to work at a school, helping the workers update their medical abilities. They are protestant, but their facilities are an old Catholic mission near the border."

"How come you know they need help?"

"The headmistress there is an old friend of my sponsor."

Jimmy's eyes widened, and he gulped down a mouthful of beans. "You have a sponsor? What's a sponsor exactly?"

Rebekah slipped her bare feet beneath the woolen blanket as she laid down. "Those are enough questions for one night, just Jimmy. Let's get some sleep before dawn."

She heard a soft snore and realized it was her own.

CHAPTER 11

Sleeping on a hard floor didn't come easier with age. Rebekah stretched gingerly and pushed herself to her feet. The floor had felt better than the chair, and once she stretched a few more times, she found her back was less painful than she thought it would be after getting caught in a flash flood. The hard floor turned out good for her. Alignment could do wonders for the body, as it had with Kurt Baxter.

Rebekah didn't straighten her makeshift bed so as not to disturb Jimmy, who was sprawled on the cot, snoring. He was still a growing boy who needed regular food and sleep.

Rebekah moved across the dirt floor of the dugout and out the front door into the blue-gray dawn of morning. Pulling the brown coat tighter around her in the chilly morning, she took a brisk walk, working out the kinks in her muscles and allowing the snap of cold air to awaken her fully.

Soon, she headed back toward the dugout but halted, her breath leaving her.

The sun peeked over the eastern rim of the canyon behind her, bathing the Palo Duro in colors Rebekah had never seen before. Russet reds lined with dusty golds ignited a feeling in her being she hadn't experienced in some time. Natural wonder and beauty weren't on her usual route through cities and shantytowns where she helped the less fortunate.

In that moment, she felt like an unfortunate for having never beheld this sight. A song rose in her heart. It was like a familiar tune, but one she'd forgotten the words to.

She stood in awe as the sun made incremental moves at a great distance to change the sight before her each passing moment. Royal purple topped the rim, then tinted the multihued layers under the bluing sky. A red-tailed hawk swooped through the canyon, its high call echoing up to her. The sandstone formations before her moved with the rhythm of her heart's song, a symphony of sight and sound.

A tear rolled down Rebekah's cheek, jolting her from the mesmerizing scene. She wiped it away and headed for the dugout, understanding how this harsh land drew its many cultures.

Inside, Jimmy was still asleep. But it was daylight and time to get a move on. She considered the best way to wake him without him coming up with fists swinging in case that was his habit from his days of growing up in the swamps of Florida. Wherever had he gotten such a tall tale?

Rebekah shook his shoulder, prepared to spring back if she needed to. But Jimmy groaned and rolled to his other side, his sandy hair flowing over his eyes.

"Jimmy?" She poked him in the back. "Just Jimmy, if you don't get out of that bed now, I'm going to eat your last can of beans."

Though she meant it teasingly, Rebekah was surprised when Jimmy bounced off the cot and landed on his feet, his long fingers raking his hair back out of his eyes. He winced and grabbed his shoulder. "Aw now, Doc, you wouldn't do that to an invalid, would you?"

"Only if that invalid is in the habit of playing possum."

They divided the last can of Jimmy's beans, and Rebekah examined his shoulder again before announcing him fit for their hike. When she asked him how long it would take, he responded by launching into a lengthy narrative on the canyon's logistics, how it was eight hundred feet deep and stretch six miles across in most places.

She urged him to get to the point, and he concluded with, "I reckon it depends on how big of a circle we want to make, which depends on how scared you are of Clem Baxter."

Rebekah gave him a look that made him wave his hands in front of him. "Never mind. It's too bad Clem doesn't realize how scared he should be of you."

"Let's just get out of this canyon, shall we?"

"You sure talk fancy, Miss Rebekah. I like it."

Jimmy still had his six-gun and carried Rebekah's medical bag. She flipped her hair up under the hat he had given her at the ranch to keep it out of the way during the hike. She chose to wear the large brown coat for the morning. Once the day warmed, she'd remove it, but for now, wearing was easier than carrying it, especially since she needed to watch where she put her bare feet.

Jimmy led the way down to the canyon floor from where they were midway up the east wall. Canyon City lay to the west. They were on the wrong side.

He kept looking around, observing their surroundings for danger. Namely, Clem and Van Baxter.

Would those two really bother hunting them down with two injured brothers back at the ranch house? Rebekah had no doubt they would. Or they could come looking for another fight with the Lowells. She trusted Jimmy's instincts as they wove their way down the deeply worn cattle trail.

They came to the creek again, which Jimmy called Palo Duro Creek. He said it flowed to the Prairie Dog Town Fork of the Red River in the canyon. Traces of the flash flood was evident in the fresh debris pushed along the edges of the creek. With the intensity of the sun bearing down on them already, Rebekah knew that in a few days, the tumble of mesquite and juniper branches would look as though they had baked there for decades.

They crossed the high creek much further down than they'd been last night and headed up the other side. Rebekah took care of where she stepped to avoid sharp-edged rocks on her bare feet. Jimmy topped the edge before her and turned, reaching down to help her the rest of the way.

She'd just clenched his hand when the report of a rifle echoed through the canyon.

The bullet struck a rock between them, splintering it mere inches from Rebekah. She yanked on Jimmy's hand, pulling him down into the creek bed. There was no place to hide above, and a quick glance around told her there was no place to hide below either.

Jimmy released her hand and went for his gun, but she grabbed his forearm and held him still.

"If they had wanted to shoot us, they would have," she said.

Jimmy, hand on the gun, glanced around wildly, shifting so that he was between her and the direction the shot came from. As they hunched on the sloped wall of the creek bed, Rebekah glanced over his shoulder and spotted a face half-hidden behind one of the rocks closer to the canyon wall. Her eyes did a sweep to see there were several faces. None of them belong to Clem or Van.

A voice shouted, "Throw your gun away!"

Jimmy's head jerked in that direction, and Rebekah caught a glimpse of his face that told him he recognized the voice.

"It's the Lowells."

CHAPTER 12

"D o as they say," Rebekah spoke quietly.

Jimmy glanced at her, eyes wide. She shook her head.

"We wouldn't stand a chance in a gunfight in the open like this," she said. "It's time to talk."

Jimmy sighed and slowly withdrew his six-gun by the butt and gave it a little toss. It was within grabbing range if they needed it, and he had her medical bag by his feet.

"Hands up!"

Jimmy straightened awkwardly, keeping his balance on the slope, hands raised. Rebekah mimicked him, though she was hidden mainly by Jimmy. She glanced behind her to see yet more faces that morphed into bodies. She and Jimmy were soon surrounded by a dozen men with Winchesters, worn jackets and hats, and tired eyes.

She identified the leader as he pushed closer to them by three steps. His face was set in a hard line, as unbending and unforgiving as the granite rock he stood by.

"You two fellows from the Baxter Ranch?"

Jimmy shifted, hands still up. "You're Sam Lowell, ain't you? I was working—"

"They're from the Baxters, all right!"

This came from a younger man who stood a few feet to the left of the leader. He glanced at the leader and said confidently, "I seen this one with those stinking Baxters when they came to run us off that time you got in a fight with Clem."

Jimmy quickly said, "The Baxters didn't have a right to—"

"Shut up," said the leader, Sam Lowell, his Winchester aimed at Jimmy's chest. "If you rode with them, you're as guilty for what they did as any. That rockslide killed my brother."

"Enough talk!" This from a man somewhere behind Rebekah. "I came to hunt Baxters, and I say we hang these two right now."

The words were so outrageous, Rebekah froze in disbelief when Sam Lowell nodded.

"Get some rope."

Rebekah sensed Jimmy coil and prepare to spring for his gun. She grabbed the back of his collar, choking him when he shifted forward.

"They won't hang us, but they will shoot you dead," she said quietly.

Hands seized her from behind, yanking her up and onto the ground above the creek. Three other men converged on Jimmy. He fought them as they dragged him up and toward a sturdy old willow tree, the only thing with suitable height to hang someone from.

One of the men had Rebekah by the arm. He slung her around and to the ground. She hit hard, her hat flying off and her hair falling over her shoulders and face.

The canyon went silent. Rebekah pushed herself up and turned to face where Sam Lowell had come through the creek and stood 20 feet from her, mouth agape.

She said, "While I deeply regret the death of your brother,

that does not give you leave to lynch a woman who was held captive at the Baxter Ranch."

Sam Lowell took another step toward her, his surprise turning to a scowl.

"Who are you?"

"Doctor Rebekah LaRoche, known in some parts as Doc Beck."

She pointed to Jimmy, who was frozen with two men latched onto him from each side. "This young man used to work for the Baxters. That changed the night he helped me escape. Please release him. He's already injured."

Sam Lowell looked between her and Jimmy, then around at the men who waited for his next command. She could tell they respected him, unlike Clem with his brothers. He looked back to the man holding Jimmy and nodded. They released Jimmy and stepped away. The boy rubbed his sore shoulder and gave Rebekah a look that said, *I'm okay.*

Sam Lowell approached her, Winchester still gripped with two hands, ready to turn and fire if needed.

"You say you're a doctor? We got a hurt man back at the settlement. Let's go."

Rebekah didn't move. "I'll treat him on your word that the boy and I will be released afterward."

Lowell flicked a glance at Jimmy, and she could see the hatred smoldering in his eyes.

"You take care of Billy, and we'll talk about it."

"Nothing doing. I want your word."

Sam Lowell stared her down, then nodded. "You have my word."

CHAPTER 13

It wasn't a long walk to the section on the west wall where the Lowells had established a home place. Surrounded on three sides by pinnacles and a mesa, it was like pulling on a glove for protection.

Rebekah scanned the walls as they entered, spotting more faces tucked in various points of the rocks, keeping watch. If the Baxters rode into this place, they were as good as dead.

A host of casitas—small adobe houses—were scattered around in a pattern that spoke of the people that once lived there. The Lowells had repaired damaged structures and built corrals for their sheep. And it wasn't this one family alone. By her estimate, Rebekah guessed about 40 people were turning this cut out of the canyon into a community. There was access to the rim for trips into town for supplies. It could be easily defended and held enough resources to make it a home.

As they walked through the center of the dwellings, Rebekah asked Jimmy, "Is this the spot the Baxters and Lowells are fighting over?"

He had her bag in his left hand. "No, ma'am. There's another section about a quarter of a mile from here, on around Timber

Mesa. It has a spring and lots of blue grama and buffalo grass. The Lowells want to run their sheep there during the spring. The Baxters were going to use it for their cattle. But they lost half their herd from disease over the winter. They still claim that section."

Rebekah wasn't interested in asking who the ownership truly belonged to. People had been battling through this canyon for decades. The mighty Comanche Nation probably knew it the best during that century, but the centuries before and the centuries ahead, who knew?

Sam Lowell ordered two men to take Jimmy to one of the corrals, where stalls were set up, and secure him there. Jimmy handed over her medical bag with a knowing grin before Lowell led Rebekah into one of the casitas.

Inside, the air was pleasantly cooler, and Rebekah paused to let her eyes adjust after the bright sunshine. Lowell hung his rifle over the mantle and nodded toward a second room. She entered through the blanket doorway and halted. A woman sat by the bedside of a poor boy no more than 13 years old as he lay on his back, sweating profusely.

Rebekah glanced sharply at Sam Lowell. "I thought you said one of your men was hurt. This is a boy."

"Boys become men fast here in Texas. Have to in order to survive. This is my only son, Billy. My wife, here."

The woman glared at him. "I told you not to take him that night! I told you..."

The boy moaned, "Ma! Ma, Pa, don't fight."

Rebekah moved to his other side and set her bag on a three-legged stool there. She pressed the back of her hand to his hot forehead, then stroked it.

"Billy, I'm a doctor, and I'll be taking care of you."

The boy whimpered when Rebekah pulled back the blanket to see the bandage on his calf. His leg was swollen, and Rebekah had a feeling she knew what she would find under the bandage.

"Mrs. Lowell, could you get me some hot water and clean cloth?"

The woman pressed a hand over her mouth and left the room, roughly pushing past her husband.

Rebekah opened her bag, but she knew what she needed had been lost in the flash flood. She spoke to Sam Lowell behind her.

"Do you have alcohol of any kind?"

"I would never let my boy drink."

Rebekah turned. "That is wise. But I need something to sterilize the wound. Surely someone in this community has some sort of medical supplies. Accidents happen all the time."

"This was no accident."

She sighed. How well she knew. "Be that as it may, please get me something to sterilize this wound."

Sam Lowell didn't take his eyes off her for several seconds. "I want my boy to come out of this all right, you understand, doctor?"

Rebekah halted from unraveling the soiled bandage and looked up at him. "There are two things I understand in this situation, Mr. Lowell. One, that your son is injured, and I need the proper tools to treat him. Two, that you are behaving exactly like Clem Baxter."

Sam Lowell's eyes widened and he opened his mouth, but snapped it shut at the sound of another moan from Billy. He stalked out of the room.

Rebekah finished unwrapping the bandage to reveal what she had suspected—infection was setting in.

Mrs. Lowell returned and thankfully didn't flinch at the sight of the puss and redness on her son's leg. She served as Rebekah's assistant as she cleaned the wound with hot water.

Sam Lowell returned shortly with a bottle of whiskey that another family had stored among their goods. Rebekah sanitized the wound before she lanced and re-bandaged it. She glanced up at Lowell, who was in the doorway.

"I need my friend to hunt down some plants for me," she said. "They were growing near where we camped last night."

Lowell narrowed his eyes. "I'll send one of my men for what you need."

Rebekah frowned. "Jimmy will not run off anywhere without me. You can trust him more than I can trust one of your men to get what I need for your son. Now, please send for him."

It was a battle of wills, same as it had been with Clem Baxter, though neither man would ever acknowledge how much they were alike.

Sam Lowell finally took a step back and turned his head to call out the door of the house, "Andy! Bring that boy in here."

Minutes later, Jimmy appeared, looking relieved to see Rebekah.

"Need my help, Doc Beck?"

"Yes, Jimmy, I need you to hunt down an aloe vera plant. There was one growing by the dugout. Bring me two thick leaves. Then stop at that willow tree where Mr. Lowell wanted to hang us and get some small branches from it. Please hurry."

Jimmy nodded and dashed out, not even looking at Lowell for permission to leave. She appreciated his loyalty to her in the few days they'd known each other but would warn him later to keep his wits about him at all times.

❦

TIME PASSED SLOWLY. Mrs. Lowell went into the kitchen of the two-room casita and began preparing the noon meal. Sam Lowell poked his head into the room where Rebekah maintained vigilance over Billy, watching the rise and fall of the young boy's chest as he struggled to breathe through the fever.

A ruckus sounded, along with a gunshot. Rebekah jumped up and ran outside behind Mrs. Lowell and others who stood outside their dwellings to see what was going on.

Jimmy was making a beeline for the casita despite the shouting of one of the guards. Sam Lowell appeared from a corral and shouted back, telling the man to stand down.

Jimmy skidded to a halt in front of the casita and held up both hands filled with willow branches, aloe vera leaves bulging from his pockets. "Got it, Doc. Anything else you need?"

Rebekah released a shaky breath. "I need you to not get yourself killed."

Jimmy shrugged and leaned over to whisper, "These fellows can't shoot for sour apples, Miss Rebekah."

"I disagree, but be that as it may, please be careful."

Rebekah took the material from him and went back inside, Jimmy following her. Mrs. Lowell had gone back into the bedroom to watch over her son.

Rebekah spread the branches on the table and took a knife from her belt where it had been hidden. Jimmy chuckled at the sight of it. Rebekah set about peeling the bark to reveal the green layer she wanted. She stripped the green as slivers in a bowl on the table, measured two tablespoons worth, and dropped them into boiling water on the stove.

Jimmy watched her, head cocked. "What are you making there?"

"Willow tea," she said. "It will help bring Billy's fever down and relieve the pain."

"They teach you that in medical school?"

"It's an old Indian remedy."

"How did you learn it?"

"I know some old Indians."

After it boiled awhile, Rebekah strained the tea and let it cool before taking a cup into the bedroom. She helped Billy drink all of the liquid, then unwrapped the bandage and applied the aloe vera gel she'd extracted from the leaves to the wound. It looked better from her earlier treatment, but he wasn't out of the woods yet.

The day wore on into the evening, and Rebekah faced the knowledge that she would yet again have an awkward night's sleep far from her lovely room at the Garland home or a hotel like she expected in Zapata. Mrs. Lowell did lay out a heavy woolen blanket similar to the one she used in the line cabin in the living room, and Rebekah negotiated to have Jimmy allowed to stay in the casita.

Sam Lowell pulled the curtain of the bedroom closed with a warning look at Rebekah and Jimmy to not try and run off. Rebekah ignored it as she laid down on the floor. At least she could stretch out and not have watch duty over a patient at last. And for the first time in days, she was safe from the Baxters.

CHAPTER 14

Mrs. Lowell served Rebekah and Jimmy a hearty breakfast of scrambled eggs and hot biscuits. It must have been her way of thanking the two for her own son's appetite and broken fever. Rebekah enjoyed every morsel of the simple affair. Mrs. Lowell also gave Rebekah a dress a size too large, but clean clothing was appreciated, along with a pair of lady's boots. The Lowells' resources were in short supply, especially with the Baxter war.

Rebekah tended her patient one last time and gave instructions to Mrs. Lowell. The woman offered her a hug before she departed.

Outside in the morning sunshine, Jimmy waited for Rebekah by their horses. She hadn't known until breakfast that the Lowell bunch had found the horses, one of them with the Baxter brand, after the flash flood. They were keeping them in a back corral. She imagined they'd planned to keep them permanently, but Sam Lowell seemed to want to do the right thing.

Lowell stood by her horse while Jimmy held the reins for both, keeping an eye on the man. Jimmy spoke to Rebekah from the side of his mouth as she approached.

"Doc, they won't give me my gun back."

Rebekah narrowed her eyes at Sam Lowell, but he didn't budge. He said, "The boy's lucky to get out of here alive after riding with the Baxters. His gun will be in Canyon City for him later if he wants it."

Rebekah started to demand he give them all their property, but she held back. The man was still grieving from the loss of his brother caused by the Baxters. This was one battle she would let go of.

She gave Jimmy a nod. "Let's mount up, Jimmy. Our work here is finished."

He sighed in resignation and took her bag from her. He tied it to her saddle while Rebekah mounted. She did miss the free ease of wearing trousers, but the skirt was plenty large enough for her to ride astride modestly.

Sam Lowell stepped back, keeping a wary eye on them.

"Tell the sheriff in Canyon City what really happened. He wasn't much interested in hearing our side of it. He's got no love for the Baxters, but none for sheep ranchers either. And...thanks."

She settled in the saddle and nodded at Lowell. "I will. And you're welcome."

She pulled the horse's head around and gave him a squeeze with her legs to pick up a trot through the Lowell settlement, Jimmy behind her. She glanced up at the guards. They didn't smile or wave farewell. Rebekah was fine with that as long as they weren't shooting at them.

Once they were through, Rebekah kept up the trot until they were a few hundred yards away from the opening, then pulled up. She turned in the saddle to speak as Jimmy came alongside her.

"Just Jimmy, it seems we've survived another scrape. Why don't we get on out of this canyon and to town now?"

Jimmy let out his breath as though he'd been holding it in for hours. He pushed his tan Stetson up to show a puff of his sandy hair.

"You sure know how to handle yourself, Miss Rebekah."

"We make a good team."

Jimmy grinned. "By golly, we do. Come on. Town's about 15 miles over the rim of Devil's Tombstone."

Rebekah let her horse follow Jimmy's at a leisurely pace. They were both still sore from their rambunctious adventures in the canyon, and taking it easy over the rocky terrain was wise for the horses. They crossed what Jimmy called Sunday Creek and followed the base of Timber Mesa.

Rebekah spied a trail right before Jimmy started guiding his horse to it. It looked like a switchback going to the top, at least from what she could see. And it looked ancient, even more so than the cattle trail on Brushy Butte. But she knew how dramatically the terrain of the canyon could change with cataclysmic events.

They started up the trail. As she maneuvered her horse around the first sharp turn, nose to tail with Jimmy's horse, Rebekah glanced to look back over Sunday Creek in the distance. She pulled her horse up to a stop and backed him a few steps for a better look, holding her breath.

Jimmy halted. "Something wrong, Doc?"

Rebekah didn't look at him, just held up her hand to keep him quiet.

Two men were riding hard from the east, cutting through the center of the canyon, heading for them. Their determined seats in the saddle and reckless flight revealed their identities.

Clem and Van Baxter.

CHAPTER 15

"L et's ride!" Jimmy called, but Rebekah motioned him to stillness again.

She looked beyond him, to the top of the canyon wall. They wouldn't be able to make it to the rim before the Baxters were within rifle range.

There was little cover on the switchback trail. At the opposite end of it from where Rebekah and Jimmy were, she saw something in the rock face that caught her attention. She nosed her horse around Jimmy on the narrow trail. This was indeed an ancient one.

"Follow me," she said.

Jimmy looked hesitant, his hand going over the empty spot where his six-gun usually would be. Then he nodded, and she urged her horse up the trail, mindful of a washed-out area and rock debris that had nearly closed it off in one place.

When they reached the rock face, Rebekah looked back to see Clem and Van at the base of the trail, drawing rifles. Eyes forward again, she pushed the horse over the last rise to level ground as the report of a rifle sounded.

Hot lead whizzed by Rebekah's ear. She hunched over in the

saddle and pushed her horse under the high rock overhang. She spared a glance behind her to see Jimmy doing the same.

They clattered into the cavern-like space. A look around confirmed her guess. This was an open rock shelter used for centuries by the first people of the land.

The ground was too hard for the shod horses' feet. Rebekah dismounted and untied her medical bag from the saddle. Jimmy hopped off his horse and grabbed her horse's reins.

"How did you know this was here, Doc? I couldn't see it from back on the trail."

"We can chat later, Jimmy. Right now, please take the horses to the other end. See if you can create a makeshift corral for them. Stay with them and remain quiet."

Rebekah retraced her steps to the opening of the shelter that ran lengthwise, facing the canyon. Staying low, she peered out to see Clem and Van making a mad dash by horseback straight up the steep slope rather than following the switchback trail.

It proved too much for Van's palomino and his riding abilities. With a terrified scream, his horse lost its footing and flipped backward. Van kicked loose of the stirrups and jumped away as the horse made a complete roll.

Dust sprayed, and the horse got to its shaky legs, standing sideways against the steepness. Van lay still on the ground not far away.

Clem didn't stop.

Rebekah loosed her medical bag from the rope Jimmy had used to secure it and spread it open wide. She pushed her few instruments and bottles to the side and popped open the false bottom. Pulling it back, she stared at the Sharps & Hankins breechloading pepperbox tucked inside.

Do no harm.

The Hippocratic oath echoed in her mind, one she'd had to check herself with in the often wild territories that her duties led her into.

She touched the cold metal of the small, four-barreled pistol and thought about praying. But there wasn't time.

It wasn't doing harm to save an innocent boy's life, nor her own.

Rebekah pulled out the pepperbox, a .32 caliber rimfire, and straightened to ease herself deeper into the rock shelter. Clem would be there within a minute. She took a precious few seconds to study her surroundings and make her decision.

The front of the shelter was broad like a road running in front of houses. The section where homes would be was formed in natural shapes that lent themselves to shelter. She went to one and discovered it opened into a comfortably sized living space with three rock walls. There was even a carved ledge like a window.

This was where Rebekah chose to position herself.

Clatter from down the way told her Jimmy wasn't going to obey her last order for him to stay with the horses. Her stomach knotted tighter.

She hissed, "Jimmy! In here."

Jimmy dodged through the opening. His eyes widened at the sight of the pistol. There was something about seeing it out and in Rebekah's hand that shocked him.

"Let me, Miss Rebekah. I'm a good shot."

"So am I, Jimmy. Now please stay behind me, out of the line of fire."

Jimmy gulped, whether from fear of her being in the line of fire or uncertainty of her ability to protect them both, she didn't know. She turned her attention to the opening that led into the ancient rock shelter, cocking the hammer on her pepperbox, licking her lips to moisten them, tasting the red clay of the canyon.

It amazed her that Clem had tracked them so far, that he hadn't given up and returned to the ranch house to care for his two wounded brothers. If he put that determination toward something worthy rather than vengeance, he could make quite a place of the Baxter Ranch.

Horse's hooves clattering along the same path she and Jimmy had taken minutes before alerted her of Clem's exact position. Rebekah used the ledge to brace against as she took aim and waited.

An eternity slipped through her mind in a single moment when Clem Baxter rode into the cave, six-gun drawn, cocked, and pointed to the ceiling as he looked around. He hadn't shaved in days, adding to his wild look. That was all Rebekah observed as she squeezed off a round.

The bullet hit its mark, the ceiling right above Clem Baxter's head. Rock sprayed over him as his horse reared in surprise, adding to the booming echoes that reverberated through the rock shelter. Clem's gun discharged. He lost his balance and rolled off. He hit the rock floor.

His horse turned and galloped outside as Clem kept rolling. He recovered and darted to the ledge of the shelter on the canyon wall.

Rebekah fired again, striking him in the leg. Clem cursed and continued his scramble up and over the ledge, disappearing from sight.

Rebekah felt a twinge of regret and relief that she had chosen not to take Clem's life when she could have. Relief because she never wanted to see anyone die. Regret because it might have cost her and Jimmy their lives.

She had two shots left. It could take more than that to bring down a wounded, mad animal.

CHAPTER 16

The echoes settled down to quiet along with the gray-brown dust. Then Clem Baxter's voice echoed violently through the rock shelter.

"You think you've won, Doc!" His words were slurred. How much had he been drinking? "I got something to tell you. No one wins against Clem Baxter. They always bend to my will, even if it kills them."

She wondered if he could see Van's still form on the side of the wall.

Rebekah debated responding, but she knew his talk was a trick. He would try to maneuver around to where he could get a bead on her.

She watched the last place she had seen him disappear into, then all along the ledge. She caught a flash of his barrel seconds before he shot, and pulled away. But the bullet ricocheted off the back wall, and Jimmy howled behind her.

Rebekah quickly looked to see him frozen against the dusty gray rock wall, eyes wide with the look of death.

"Jimmy," she whispered, voice choked with tears.

He blinked and turned his head toward her. His eyes kept moving to the little hole in the rock beside his head.

Rebekah closed her eyes in relief, gulped, then looked back to the outside. Clem Baxter was scrambling over the ledge. He was at an angle that Rebekah couldn't get a clear shot at. He dove into an opening further down.

He was getting around well despite the hole in his leg. She could have shot out his kneecap and crippled him for life. She would likely regret not doing that as well. He could still shoot straight despite the alcohol in his blood.

It was time to end this.

Rebekah unloaded the two remaining cartridges in her pepperbox.

Jimmy whispered hoarsely, "Doc, what are you doing?"

"Hush."

Rebekah slid the barrel back in place and cocked the hammer in the stillness. She squeezed the trigger.

Click.

She cocked and squeezed it again. And again, rapidly. Click. Click, click!

A deadly laugh sounded from not more than a dozen yards away.

"Maybe you'd like to talk now, Doc? Trouble is, I'm not in the mood for talking."

While the words echoed in the rock shelter, Rebekah reloaded her two cartridges and cocked the hammer. Clem Baxter was stepping into the roadway of the shelter, gun out and aimed at her enclosure, moving forward as he dragged his leg along.

"You're going to regret ever crossing me, lady."

Rebekah pressed herself against the wall, her gun down, out of sight. Clem Baxter hadn't spotted her yet. She raised the pepperbox and took aim.

A shout came from the other end of the rock shelter.

"Drop it, Clem!"

Rebekah's eyes scanned the darkness behind Clem. Clem did, too, firing his gun as he turned. A single shot answered, knocking Clem Baxter flat on his back.

Rebekah slowly released the breath she'd been holding and uncocked her pistol.

Sam Lowell appeared on the roadway, walking up toward Clem Baxter, Winchester in hand. Several other men appeared out of the rocks. Lowell men.

Sam Lowell came to a stop over Clem's body. He looked toward where Rebekah and Jimmy were.

"You all right, Doc Beck?"

Rebekah finished releasing her breath and straightened off the wall so that he could see her through the opening.

"We are well."

She and Jimmy joined Lowell. The man glanced down at her hand, taking in the pepperbox.

"You arrived just in time, Mr. Lowell," Rebekah said.

"We followed you and the boy from our place, wanted to make sure you left," Lowell said. "When we saw the Baxter boys riding into the canyon, we decided to keep a watch and see if what you told us was true. When we heard you out of bullets, figured it was time to step in."

Jimmy chuckled, a dry, choked sound. "Oh, Doc Beck had two—"

Rebekah put a hand on his arm, and he looked at her questioningly but said nothing else. He didn't know why she didn't want him to say she had ammunition left. She wasn't sure why either, other than she wanted Sam Lowell to know that she meant what she had said. He stepped into action just in time.

Although she knew the answer, Rebekah squatted beside Clem Baxter and pressed two fingers against his neck, feeling for a pulse. There was none. He had died instantly from the bullet that struck his heart.

Someone called from the direction of the switchback trail. "This other Baxter, he's coming to."

The group went outside and Rebekah saw Van Baxter sitting up, holding his head with one hand, the rifles of two Lowell men trained on him.

He glanced up, wincing. Blood ran down one side of his face from the reopened cut above his temple, along with a new one. Rebekah had seen the blood of all four Baxter brothers.

She came to a stop before Van, who glared at her without speaking.

"Van, I'm sorry to have to tell you this, but your brother is dead."

Van's eyes glazed over with anger, pain, and back to anger. He lunged to his feet. "You...it's all your fault!"

"No, Van, it is not my fault, nor anyone else here," Rebekah said. "Your brother made his choices. Now it's up to you to make yours. I suggest you go home, bury your brother, and listen to Woodrow. He's the oldest of the Baxter sons now."

Sam Lowell scooped Van's hat off the ground and slapped it into the young man's chest. "I would take the doc's advice. She's a smart lady."

CHAPTER 17

"Jimmy, he is a good boy."

These words came from Mrs. Cuesta in Spanish as Rebekah helped her make corn tortillas for the evening meal.

After they saw the sheriff in Canyon City and sent a telegram to Doctor McKinnon in Wyoming, Jimmy had assured Rebekah that he had the perfect place for them to spend the night before going north to Amarillo. She still had a train to catch.

The Cuestas lived in a casita outside Canyon City with their eight children in ages varying from infant to twelve years old. Rebekah appreciated stepping into this large, joyful family after the long few days. She had no complaints about sharing a bed with three of the little girls, though she did look forward to the moment she had a private bedroom for a night.

Rebekah pressed out a corn tortilla with the palm of her hand. "How long have you known Jimmy?" she asked Mrs. Cuesta in Spanish.

Jimmy was in the living room of the open space, howling like a mad dog as he galloped on all fours, chasing two of the littlest

Cuesta children. They squealed and jumped in their father's lap. Mrs. Cuesta smiled at the commotion.

"Jimmy helped carry my goods and children from the store in town one day, a year ago. He comes every week to our home after church. That boy, he never misses services."

"He goes to your church?"

Mrs. Cuesta laughed, barely heard above the squeals. "He goes to every church."

Rebekah laid the tortilla in the sizzling oil. It was the last one before the family settled at the table.

Mr. Cuesta prayed in Spanish, blessing the food before the table erupted in chatter again. Jimmy did a lot of grinning, which Rebekah found amusing. She learned he could hardly speak a word of Spanish.

The Cuestas tried to direct some of the conversation in English, but it was a difficult language for them. Rebekah wasn't as fluent in Spanish as she wished she were, and found herself smiling along with Jimmy when she couldn't grasp the words flying around. Mr. Cuesta finally rapped his knuckles on the plank table.

He cleared his throat and said in English, "We will let the guests speak. Doctor, tell us why you would go to New Mexico Territory?"

Rebekah decided to answer in English to include Jimmy in the conversation. "I am going to visit the girls' school, Hope Academy, to instruct the teachers there on some of the latest medical practices. They do much of their own nursing and..."

Rebekah didn't finish as her words registered on the Cuestas' faces.

Mrs. Cuesta put a hand to her throat, and Mr. Cuesta said gravely, "The school is no good place for you to go. Banditos have taken it over and threaten to slaughter all inside."

Jimmy coughed while Rebekah's eyes widened. She asked, "What about the local law enforcement?"

"They not get in. Mexican Army not get in. You not get in."

Rebekah looked between the husband and wife. "I must go."

Those were the words simplest for the Cuestas, Jimmy, and her to comprehend.

Mr. Cuesta nodded solemnly. "We will pray for you. You will take Jimmy, *sí*?"

Rebekah raised an eyebrow. "I don't think that's a good..."

Jimmy banged his fist on the table, making the children jump. "I'll go with you, Doc Beck! You can count on me."

⚜

LATE THAT EVENING, Rebekah went through the front room on the way to the small bedroom where the girls slept. She'd gone out for fresh air after everyone settled in for the night and was returning to see if she could find a spot on the bed that the girls shared.

Passing by the adobe fireplace where Jimmy had a bedroll, she heard him whisper, "Miss Rebekah? You going to bed now?"

"I was."

"Can we talk a spell?"

Rebekah was thoroughly exhausted and knew a long day of traveling lay ahead, but she relented to Jimmy's request and sat on a low stool. She owed him a great deal, and there was something she needed to speak with him about, too.

He propped himself up on one elbow. "What do you think about what the Cuestas said about that girls' school?"

"I haven't given it a great deal of thought yet. Once I get to the town, I'll be able to assess the situation."

Jimmy shook his head, his boyish look of amazement overtaking his expression.

"Like Sam Lowell said, you sure are a smart lady, all them fancy words. You got to stay at the Victoria Hotel sometime. You'd be impressed. They have a two-story outhouse that's as fine as anything you've seen. You see, when someone uses the upstairs—"

Rebekah held her hand up straight in front of Jimmy, stopping him.

"Really, Jimmy. Really."

He was so wide-eyed innocent. She shook her head with a soft chuckle.

"What I was thinking about outside was you and how you might need someone to finish raising you," she said. "Now I'm sure of it. How would you like to come along with me not only to Zapata but beyond? I have other work yet, but will eventually return to Wyoming. I have a job I can get you at a fine ranch if you're interested."

Jimmy's eyes widened with his grin. "Would you really, Doc?"

"I would really, but you have to promise me something."

"What's that?"

"That you never again talk about two-story outhouses."

"Deal."

Jimmy raised enough to give her hand a hard shake, then cocked his head in curiosity.

"Wyoming. That where your home is, Miss Rebekah?"

She hesitated, then decided to be fully honest. "That's something I ask myself often, just Jimmy."

Wyoming was a place she hoped Jimmy could call home. She had a feeling he needed one, the same as everyone did. Her real one was so very, very far out of reach.

But if she could help people like Jimmy and Kurt and Billy and whoever else needed her, her plight was worth it.

Dearest reader,

Thank you for reading *Canyon War (Doc Beck Westerns Book 1)*. I truly hope it entertained and delighted you!

If you fell in love with the main characters, Rebekah, aka "Doc Beck," and Jimmy, you'll be excited to know book 2, *Mission Bandits*, is now available! You can order it on any major retail site or through www.SarahElisabethWrites.com.

I'd also be thrilled if you took a moment to write your thoughts in the form of a review and post it on your favorite retail outlet and Goodreads. You'll help other readers find this series.

To discover more of my books, free short stories, and to generally stay in touch with me, I invite you to join my VIP reader newsletter. You'll receive a free copy of *The Executions*, book one in my historical fiction *Choctaw Tribune* Series. Please join me through:

www.subscribepage.com/sarahelisabethwrites_choctaw-tribune-book-one.

Speaking of history, the character of Doc Beck was inspired by Dr. Susan La Flesche (Omaha), who is hailed as the first American Indian to earn a medical degree. In continued research, my mother found Dr. Isabel Cobb (Cherokee), the first woman physician in Indian Territory, in very nearly the same years as Dr. La Flesche.

Lastly, if you're not familiar with my heritage books based on my Choctaw history and culture, you can check them out on www.SarahElisabethWrites.com. Questions? Please send them my way: me@sarahelisabethwrites.com

—Sarah Elisabeth Sawyer
Historical Fiction and Western author
Tribal member of the Choctaw Nation of Oklahoma

MISSION BANDITS (DOC BECK WESTERNS BOOK 2)

The Mexican army, a town marshal, and the Sancho Guerra gang are facing off when Doctor Rebekah LaRoche and her new friend, Jimmy, arrive in Zapata, New Mexico Territory. The bandits are holding hostages at Hope Academy, a school for girls located in an old mission outside of town, and Rebekah feels compelled to act—she was sent to the school to modernize the infirmary, not see the innocent occupants murdered.

The notorious and charismatic bandit, Sancho Guerra, led his band of men on a pillaging spree from Mexico to the mission and has proven his indifference to killing, prepared for any tricks the army or the Zapata town marshal throw at him.

But he isn't prepared for Rebekah, and now the Mexican army colonel wants her to do something terrifying—enter the mission and help with the capture of the deadliest men in the territory.

***Mission Bandits* is available on multiple retailer sites.**

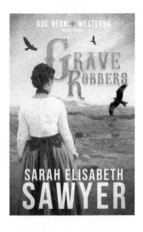

"You swing just as high for killing one as you do three."

Called on to perform an autopsy for a murder case, Doctor Rebekah LaRoche and Just Jimmy find themselves as unlikely detectives in a town with too many secrets.

One of the bandits who held the old mission and Rebekah hostage is accused of murdering Ruby Palmer, a young woman who took some of those secrets with her in death. When Rebekah discovers them during the autopsy, she must fight to prove her former captor is innocent. But she soon learns truth isn't something this town welcomes.

There isn't one straight shooter in the lot—the corrupt sheriff, judge, and leading townsmen are ready to lynch the bandit with hardly a trial. The only man Rebekah partly trusts is Deputy Thad Biggins. But what secret is driving him?

With the whole town against her, Rebekah finds herself at a crossroads: Let the bandit guilty of many crimes hang for one he didn't commit; or prove his innocence by robbing Ruby Palmer's grave.

Grave Robbers is available on multiple retailer sites.

♦ ♦ ♦

Who would show up for their own execution?

It's 1892, Indian Territory. A war is brewing in the Choctaw Nation as two political parties fight out issues of old and new ways. Caught in the middle is eighteen-year-old Ruth Ann, a Choctaw who doesn't want to see her family killed.

In a small but booming pre-statehood town, her mixed blood family owns a controversial newspaper, the *Choctaw Tribune*. Ruth Ann wants to help spread the word about critical issues but there is danger for a female reporter on all fronts—socially, politically, even physically.

But what is truly worth dying for? This quest leads Ruth Ann and her brother Matthew, the stubborn editor of the fledgling *Choctaw Tribune*, to old Choctaw ways at the farm of a condemned murderer. It also brings them to head on clashes with leading townsmen who want their reports silenced no matter what.

More killings are ahead. Who will survive to know the truth? Will truth survive?

***The Executions* is available on multiple retailer sites.**

◆ ◆ ◆

TRAITORS (CHOCTAW TRIBUNE SERIES, BOOK 2)

"Someone's going to be king in this territory.
No reason it can't be me. It sure won't be you."

Betrayed.

Someone is tearing at the fabric of the Choctaw Nation while political turmoil, assassinations, and feuds threaten the very sovereignty of the tribe. It stands under the U.S. government's scrutiny.

When heated words turn to hot lead, Ruth Ann Teller—a mixed-blood Choctaw—fears losing her brother who won't settle for anything but the truth. Matthew is determined to use his newspaper, the *Choctaw Tribune*, to uncover the scheme behind Mayor Thaddeus Warren's claim to the townsite of Dickens. Matthew is willing to risk his newspaper—and his life—to uncover a traitor among their Choctaw people.

But when Ruth Ann tries to help, she causes more harm than good—especially after the mayor brings in Lance Fuller, a schoolteacher from New York. How does this charming yet aloof young man fit into the mayor's scheme?

When attacks against the newspaper strike and bullets fly, a trip to the Chicago World's Fair of 1893 is the answer they need to save the Choctaw Tribune. The trip holds a key to Matthew's investigation.

But Ruth Ann must find the courage to face a journey to the White City —without her brother.

***Traitors* is available on multiple retailer sites.**

♦♦♦

SHAFT OF TRUTH (CHOCTAW TRIBUNE SERIES, BOOK 3)

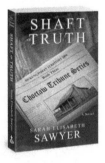

"Nothing to it but a stout heart."

On a mission to bring justice to the outlaw gang that murdered his father and brother, Matthew Teller leaves the *Choctaw Tribune* newspaper for his sister to operate and plunges into an unfamiliar world of darkness and danger. Working inside the coal mines of the Choctaw Nation—one of the most dangerous places in the country—he searches for a man who may have the answers to this six-year-old mystery. But after Matthew uncovers an earth-shattering truth that rocks him to his core, he must decide what right is, and what price he is willing to pay for it.

Ruth Ann Teller knows she can handle publishing the *Choctaw Tribune*— until she loses their biggest advertiser. Now, with Matthew miles away and the future of the newspaper resting squarely on her shoulders, Ruth Ann must make a bold move to keep the newspaper afloat in her brother's absence. She sets it on a course for new success or total disaster.

Striking coal miners. Outlaw gangs. An unsolved crime. And a Choctaw family that fights for one another, and for truth.

Shaft of Truth (_Choctaw Tribune_ Series, Book 3) is available on multiple retailer sites.

◆◆◆

ANUMPA WARRIOR: CHOCTAW CODE TALKERS OF WORLD WAR I

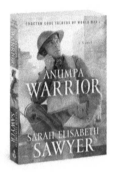

The day I betrayed Isaac, I vowed never again to speak my native language in front of white men.

When America enters the Great War in 1917, Bertram Robert Dunn and his Choctaw buddies from Armstrong Academy join the army to protect their homes, their families, and their country. Hoping to find redemption for a horrible lie that betrayed his best friend, B.B. heads into the trenches of France—but what he discovers is a duty only his native tongue can fulfill.

War correspondent Matthew Teller is ready to quit until an encounter with a fellow Choctaw sets him on a path to write the untold story of American Indian doughboys. But entrenched stereotypes and prejudices tear at his burning desire to spread truth.

With the Allies building toward the greatest offensive drive of the war, the American Expeditionary Forces face a superior enemy who intercepts their messages and knows their every move. Can the solution come from a people their own government stripped of culture and language?

Anumpa Warrior is available on multiple retailer sites.

TOUCH MY TEARS: TALES FROM THE TRAIL OF TEARS

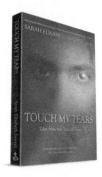

For this collection of short stories, Choctaw authors from five U.S. states came together to present a part of their ancestors' journey, a way to honor those who walked the trail for their future. These stories not only capture a history and a culture, but the spirit, faith, and resilience of the Choctaw people.

Tears of sadness. Tears of joy. Touch and experience them.

Touch My Tears is available on multiple retailer sites.

♦ ♦ ♦

TUSHPA'S STORY (Touch My Tears Collection)

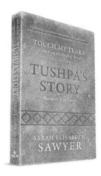

"Protect the book as you do our seed corn. We must have both to survive."

The Treaty of Dancing Rabbit Creek changed everything. The Choctaw Nation could no longer remain in their ancient homelands.

Young Tushpa, his family, and their small band embark on a trail of life and death. More death than life lay ahead.

On their journey to a new homeland, the faith of his father and one book guide Tushpa as he learns what it means to become a man and a leader.

But before long, betrayal from within and without rip at the unity of the band. Can Tushpa help keep his tattered people together? Or will they all be lost to sickness of the mind, body, and spirit on the four hundred mile walk?

A continuation of the anthology *Touch My Tears: Tales from the Trail of Tears*, this story follows an original manuscript written by Tushpa's son, James Culberson.

Tushpa's Story is available on multiple retailer sites.

ACKNOWLEDGMENTS

Every book is a work of art, but this art doesn't come about as a solo endeavor. It starts with prayer to my Father in Heaven, to Whom all praise goes.

He has surrounded me with supporters in my writing career who constantly uplift me. For this book, I want to say a special thanks to my dear friends and fellow authors, Mollie Reeder and Catherine Frappier. They never fail to show their enthusiasm for my new books, even when in the embryo stage. They also aren't shy about helping me along in the process!

When I asked for feedback on the original subpar covers I tried to create for the series, Mollie came back with a phenomenal concept, and worked with my quirks to bring it all to life. What can I say, she's an amazing creative! Check out Mollie's work at her site here.

Catherine, though slightly occupied as a Constitutional law student at Harvard University, carved out time to read the manuscript and offer editorial suggestions for this first book of a new series. She is sharp yet gentle in her analysis. You, the reader, have reaped the rewards of her intelligence as an avid reader of fiction.

I also want to thank fellow author, Natalie Bright, for her excellent feedback. She *lives and ranches* in Canyon, y'all! I so appreciated her attention to details for the Palo Duro Canyon that helped make the book authentic in its history and presentation of this natural wonder. You can find out more on her Western Romances here.

No story gets written without the ever-loving and patient support of my mama, Lynda Kay Sawyer. She's my first editor, business partner, cook, and best friend. She is a Choctaw artist in her own right (ChoctawSpirit.com) and I love her so dearly. xoxo.

Finally, I thank you, dear reader, for the constant flow of encouragement you offer through reading my stories, sending emails, and offering kind words on social media. You truly inspire me to get up in the mornings and write.

I would love to hear your thoughts on this book! Email me@sarahelisabethwrites.com to share. God bless you.

—Sarah Elisabeth

ABOUT THE AUTHOR

SARAH ELISABETH SAWYER is a story archaeologist. She digs up shards of past lives, hopes, and truths, and pieces them together for readers today. The Smithsonian's National Museum of the American Indian honored her as a literary artist through their Artist Leadership Program for her work in preserving Choctaw Trail of Tears stories. A tribal member of the Choctaw Nation of Oklahoma, she writes historical fiction from her hometown in Texas, partnering with her mother, Lynda Kay Sawyer, in continued research for future works. Learn more at SarahElisabethWrites.com, Facebook.com/SarahElisabethSawyer

Lightning Source UK Ltd.
Milton Keynes UK
UKHW010137090223
416726UK00009B/162